THE
SECRET FUNERAL
OF SLIM JIM
THE SNAKE

THE
SECRET FUNERAL
OF SLIM JIM
THE SNAKE

~~~~~~~~~~~~~~~~

Elvira Woodruff

A Yearling Book

Published by
Bantam Doubleday Dell Books for Young Readers
a division of
Bantam Doubleday Dell Publishing Group, Inc.
1540 Broadway
New York, New York 10036

ISBN: 0-440-40945-4

Reprinted by arrangement with Holiday House, Inc.

Printed in the United States of America

August 1994

10   9   8   7   6

For Tara,
who's lucky enough to have a Vincent of her own!

THE
SECRET FUNERAL
OF SLIM JIM
THE SNAKE

Chapter One

"**Y**ou live in a funeral home?" That was the first question kids asked Nick Robbins when they met him.

He would then explain that his house wasn't in the funeral home itself, but rather over it. Nick's uncle Walter was the sole proprietor of the Wiloby Funeral Home in the little town of Wiloby, Pennsylvania. Nick's parents had been killed in a car crash when he was a baby, and so he had moved in with his aunt Marge and his uncle Walter Hadley.

Nick found life at the Wiloby Funeral Home extremely boring. The scary, creepy side of the business—the embalming room—was behind the locked doors that Nick had tried to open when he was just two years old. Uncle

Walter was the only person with a key, and he never allowed anyone into the embalming room except his assistant, Vincent. When Uncle Walter wasn't working with a "client," he spent hours keeping the place up, dusting the coffins, trimming the lawn, raking the white stones that edged the big plastic WILOBY FUNERAL HOME sign out front or clipping the hedges along the driveway.

"We've got to put on our best face," Uncle Walter liked to say. His brown mustache, trimmed as neatly as his lawn, arched slightly over a thin little smile, the only kind of smile Uncle Walter allowed himself. When he was angry, his mustache dipped slightly over an equally thin frown. Everything about Uncle Walter was thin, Nick decided, thin and trim and orderly.

Unfortunately, ten-year-old Nick Robbins was just the opposite. Nick had no interest in order at all. His hair was a tangle of unbrushed blond curls, his fingernails were filled with whatever dirt was at hand, and he could never stop himself from grinning when he was happy or letting his mouth sag into a deep frown when he was sad.

"You need to learn not to display your emotions in public," Uncle Walter would scold with a little shake of his head.

On such occasions, Aunt Marge would sigh. "Nick can't help it," she'd say. "He's so like his father." Then Nick would wonder, what was my father really like?

"Well, he was nothing like your uncle Walter, I can tell you that much," Aunt Marge had whispered once. Nick noticed the twinkle in her eye as she said this. He was glad that his father wasn't like Uncle Walter, but he didn't need Aunt Marge to tell him that. He could see it for himself.

Nick loved looking at the photograph of his parents in the green frame on the mantel in the living room. It showed a blond-haired young woman with a gentle smile. Nick would stare into his mother's soft blue eyes and imagine her talking to him. Her voice was light and young, and she would always be saying the same thing.

"I've made some of your favorite cookies, Nick. There's a whole batch of peanut butter chocolate chip cookies here, just for you."

"And what about me?" Nick's father would ask. Nick would turn and gaze at the young man in the picture, whose thick unruly hair framed his smiling face. Nick loved the wide grin that stretched across his father's face. That grin told Nick that Jack Robbins had been a man who didn't give two hoots about trimming hedges or keeping his feelings from the world. It was the unmistakable wide-open grin of an adventurer, a free spirit, a long-distance truck driver.

"That's what we could never understand," Aunt Marge had said a number of times. "All those long trips your father took in his truck and never an accident, and then for it to happen when he was with your mother in a car." Aunt Marge would look away at this part, since Jack Robbins, Nick's father, had been her favorite brother. Then after a little while, she'd turn around and look at Nick again. "Thank God you were with a baby-sitter that night. You're all we have left of them."

Nick had no memory of his father or his father's truck, but he spent a good deal of his time daydreaming about both. In his dreams, Nick sat on a hard leather seat in a silver-and-blue cab. His father sat next to him, gripping the steering wheel with his strong rough hands.

"We've got a lot of road to mow down on

this trip," Jack Robbins would say with a wink. "Do you think you're up to it, son?"

"Sure, Dad," Nick would answer. Then he would reach into the glove compartment for two green lollipops. (In Nick's daydreams, Jack Robbins loved green lollipops almost as much as Nick did.) As Nick slipped two lollipops from their wrappers, he glanced down at the car in front of them. It was a station wagon and in the backseat were two boys about his age. They were pumping their arms up and down and pleading with their eyes. Perched in the cab, high above the car, Nick felt much older than the boys. He turned to his father.

"The horn, Dad," he'd say, and Jack Robbins would lift his thick muscled arm over his head and pull the wire that was strung across the top of the cab. Suddenly the loud honk of the air horn would blast across the road. Nick would gaze down at the boys while his father pulled into the fast lane. He could see the look of awe and even envy on their faces. That's when his father would step on the gas, and Nick would wave as they rode off in a cloud of dust. It was Nick's all-time favorite daydream.

On this particular Saturday morning, he had just got to the part of the dream where the dust kicks up when he heard the roar of a vacuum cleaner outside his bedroom. It was Aunt Marge sucking up what could only be the thought of dust balls in the hall, as none were ever allowed to actually form there. The vacuum died down to a low purr, and Nick could hear Aunt Marge moving down the stairs.

Nick made his way across the bedroom to the window by the bookcase. He stared out at the overpass, listening to the traffic on Route 22. He thought he heard a diesel's engine, and was ready to dip back into his daydream when the screech of a weeder-eater came from below. He looked down and saw Uncle Walter attacking the few trembling weeds that had dared to grow along the sidewalk.

Nick shrank from the window. It was only a matter of minutes before Uncle Walter would be calling him to start his summer chores— dusting the coffins, reraking the little white stones around the sign, retrimming the lawn, and reclipping the hedges. Nick flopped onto his bed with a heavy sigh. He knew that like his father, he was a man of action, made for adventure and change. How, except by some cruel quirk of fate, had he landed in the lap of order and boredom at the Wiloby Funeral Home?

He pulled a worn matchbook out of his pocket and thought about how a man of action needs a plan. Nick opened the matchbook and began to read aloud the little red print on the inside of the cover.

"Are You Dissatisfied with Your Present Job? Does your life seem Boring and Predictable? Do you like being your Own Boss? Do you long for Change, and the Adventure of seeing New Places, meeting New People? Now's the time to Act! Consider Long-Distance Trucking. With our Correspondence Course we'll train you to handle state-of-the-art rigs, and have you on that open road within two short months! Act Now! Call or write for Details. . . ." In even smaller print it said, "Must be 18 years or older."

"I wish I was eighteen years old right now," Nick sighed. He turned the match cover over and continued to read.

"A Special Close-Out Offer. For only $10.99, we'll send you *The Truckers' Road Atlas*. This specially designed atlas not only offers complete maps of all major highways in the United States, but also provides truckers with current road conditions, weigh station locales, and weight limitations on major bridges. 'No trucker should be without one,' says Brad

Robertson, trucker for TransAmerican Fruit. '*The Truckers' Road Atlas* has saved me hours of road time. I call it the truckers' bible,' reports Frank Scarponi, a Tri-Star hauler."

Nick had to squint to read the tiny print that stated the offer ended at the end of the month.

"That's only two weeks away," Nick whispered, shoving the matchbook back into his pocket. He cautiously made his way down the stairs, being careful to keep out of Aunt Marge's sight. He grabbed an apple from the kitchen counter, opened the front door, and stole out of the house. Darting behind trees, looking first backward and then forward, Nick made his way down Filmont Street. The screech of the weeder-eater coming from behind the Wiloby Funeral Home was soon no more than a faint buzz in his ear. Nick Robbins was no longer thinking about grass cutting or hedge clipping.

Nick Robbins was busy thinking up a plan, a plan to raise ten ninety-nine within the next two weeks, so that he could send away for his very own "truckers' bible."

Chapter Two

"Hi, Icky Nicky," seven-year-old Megan Persetti sang out when she opened the Persettis' front door. Nick groaned. "I told you to stop calling me that," he muttered, stepping inside. Megan's girlfriend, Tara Haley, was standing beside her. The two girls broke into a flurry of giggles.

"Where's the Bubs?" Nick called after them as they raced up the stairs.

"He's in the den, Icky Nicky," Megan called back. Nick shrugged and headed for the den.

He knew little sisters could be pesty, since along with Aunt Marge and Uncle Walter, Nick lived with his seven-year-old cousin, Emily. He called her "Em the Phlem" when she pestered him. It was she who had called

him Icky Nicky in the first place, and now
every six- and seven-year-old girl in the neighborhood was calling him that.

Nick stepped into the den. Bubs and his
sheepdog, Moose, were sitting on the couch
watching television. Bubs Persetti was Nick's
best friend. His real name was Brian, but everyone called him Bubs. He and Moose spent
a lot of time watching television. Moose especially liked the cartoons.

"Hey, Nick, how's it going?" Bubs asked,
moving over on the couch to make room for his
friend. Moose, a mountain of gray-and-white
fur, didn't budge. (He was too busy watching
a Road Runner cartoon to notice Nick.)

"Bubs, I've got this great idea," Nick began.
But before he could continue, Moose opened
his mouth in a big yawn. Bubs turned to look
inside.

"Oh, wow, look at Moose's tongue," Bubs
whispered. "It's full of little cracks, like little
rivers."

"Yeah, it's got a lot of cracks," Nick said,
looking into Moose's mouth. "Now about my
idea . . ."

"And look at those big teeth, way back
there," Bubs said, pointing to Moose's molars.

Nick took a quick look at the molars before Moose ended his yawn with a loud sigh.

"What I want to show . . ." Nick started to say.

"Did you hear that, Nick?" Bubs interrupted. "He's been doing that a lot lately. It sounds as if he's depressed, doesn't it?"

"Depressed? Well, I don't know." Nick tried to sound interested, but he was growing impatient. He was making plans for his future career and all his best friend could talk about were the cracks on his depressed dog's tongue!

"So, anyway, what I wanted to show you," Nick began again, but Bubs and Moose had turned their attention back to the television. On the screen a woman was shaking her head of long fluffy golden hair in a commercial for hair coloring. Nick wondered why Bubs was so interested in a commercial for hair dye.

"That's the stuff my mom uses," said Bubs. Nick's mouth flopped open. He was shocked to hear that his best friend's mother was not a natural redhead.

"Sometimes, a new look can change the way you feel," the lady with the lush blond hair purred from the TV. "My friends all tell me how great I look now, and that's just how I feel. Oh, this formula may be more expensive, but I'm worth it."

"And so is Moose," Bubs purred back. "Let's go."

"Huh?" Nick croaked. Bubs was heading for the bathroom, with sleepy old Moose following behind him. Nick quickly stood up.

"What are you going to do?" he demanded once they had locked themselves in the Persettis' bathroom. Bubs pointed to Moose, who was drinking out of the toilet bowl.

"I've been thinking about doing this for a while," Bubs said. "I'm going to give old Moose here a new look. Maybe then he won't be so depressed." Bubs reached for a box of hair coloring in the cabinet. "We have to be careful not to use too much, or my mom will notice it's gone," Bubs whispered. He spread out the directions on the sink counter. "OK, it says that first you need to wash the hair." He turned Moose around and dipped his tail in the toilet bowl. Moose blinked and looked behind him.

"I can't believe you're doing this," Nick said, making a face. "What if your mom comes in?"

"She won't. She's working today," Bubs told

him. Nick knew that Mrs. Persetti worked part-time as a realtor. "She's got a bunch of houses to show, so she'll be gone all morning." Bubs looked back at the box. "It says 'Auburn Rinse.' That must mean you can rinse it out. We can give Moose a new look for the morning and then rinse it off before my mom comes home."

"You're really going to dye his hair?" Nick whispered.

"They never say dye on TV," Bubs corrected him. "On TV they say 'color it.' And no, I'm not going to color all of it, just some of it, just his tail." Bubs reached for the bottle of shampoo that was on the top shelf over the tub. He poured a glob onto Moose's shaggy tail. "So what were you saying about an idea?" he asked, looking over at Nick.

"Well, you know how much I think about my dad," Nick said, sitting down on the hamper seat, "and what a great trucker he was." Bubs nodded. He worked Moose's tail into a long lathery rope of suds.

"Well," Nick continued, "I've decided to be a trucker, too. I'm going to take a course so I can learn to be a long-distance trucker, just like my dad." Nick reached into his pocket and pulled out the matchbook cover. He read the tiny print out loud.

"Read that last part to me again," Bubs said, as he pulled Moose back toward the tub and turned on the water.

" 'Must be eighteen years or older.' " Nick frowned. "I know I'll have to wait until I'm eighteen to take the course, but listen to this." He turned the match cover over and continued to read, repeating the line, " 'No trucker should be without one.' "

"All I need is ten ninety-nine and I can send away for the atlas now. If I start studying it every night, by the time I'm eighteen, I'll know every road in America."

Nick grinned. "I can feel my foot on the gas right now." He began making engine noises as he put his foot on an imaginary gas pedal. He jumped off the hamper and maneuvered his imaginary eighteen-wheeler around the tiny bathroom.

"You're the only kid I know who wants to be a truck driver," Bubs said, reaching for the box of hair coloring.

"So what?" Nick demanded, his smile suddenly fading.

"Oh, nothing," Bubs replied quickly. "It's just that most kids dream about being baseball players or race car drivers or something good like that. So how are you going to get the ten ninety-nine in only two weeks?"

"I don't know," Nick replied, coming to a stop next to the bathtub. He held up the matchbook cover.

"You spent all your birthday money on baseball cards, and Christmas is months away," Bubs reminded him.

"Do you have any money you could loan me?" Nick asked.

"I've only got seventy-nine cents saved up," Bubs reported. He poured some hair coloring onto Moose's wet tail. "And besides, I owe Meg two dollars. Maybe we could have a lemonade stand."

"We tried that last summer, don't you remember?" Nick shook his head. "We sat out in front of your house for three hours and made fifty cents. The lemonade cost us more than that. No, there's got to be another way to get the money."

"It's too bad you don't know any rich and friendly kids who would loan you the money," Bubs said as he wrapped Moose's tail in the plastic head wrap that came with the hair-coloring set.

"I do know someone who is rich, though,"

Nick said suddenly. "He may not be very friendly, but he's the richest kid in town."

"If he's not very friendly and the richest kid in town," Bubs repeated, "that's got to be . . ."

"Bernard Trauffman," Nick and Bubs said together.

"Yeah, I'd say that Bernard Trauffman is the richest and snootiest kid we know," Bubs agreed. "There's no way that he'd ever loan you the money."

"You're right, but he wouldn't have to loan it to me," Nick said with a grin.

"You're crazy if you think he'd give it to you," Bubs replied.

"Not loan it, or give it, but trade it," Nick explained. "Now all I have to do is think of something that I can trade with."

"That's going to be tricky. Bernard's got more stuff than any of us, and enough money to buy whatever he wants," said Bubs.

"So it'll have to be something that he can't get himself," Nick decided. "Something really different. You know how he loves to show off." It was true, Bernard Trauffman was never happier than when he had got something new, something that none of the other kids had. Nick's face lit up.

"Who did Bernard love the most?" he asked excitedly.

"That's easy," Bubs answered, "his snake, Slim Jim. You aren't thinking of getting him another snake, are you? Because I heard him telling Danny Miller that since Slim died yesterday, he didn't want any more pets, not for now, anyway."

"No, I wasn't thinking of getting him a new pet. I was thinking of getting him something for his old pet," Nick replied.

"His old pet? You mean his old *dead* pet?" Bubs looked confused. "What could you give a dead snake?"

"A funeral," Nick grinned. "A real funeral, right in the Wiloby Funeral Home, with flowers, and music, and . . ."

"And you'll never get away with it," Bubs interrupted. "Because your uncle Walter would never . . ."

"Would never know," Nick finished his sentence. "Grammy Robbins is coming to stay with us next weekend, while Uncle Walter and Aunt Marge go to Chicago for a casket convention. Grammy is bringing her sewing machine so she and Emily can make a bunch of clothes for Emily's dolls. The two of them will be busy sewing, Aunt Marge and Uncle Walter will be busy looking at caskets, and we'll be busy putting on the fanciest funeral a snake could ever hope for!"

"You're a genius!" Bubs whispered. He began to pull the soggy plastic wrap off Moose's tail.

"And your dog has a red tail!" Nick gasped.

Chapter Three

"He'll have a coffin, a real coffin?" Bernard Trauffman asked, his watery blue eyes growing wider every second. (Slim's remains were currently resting in an old coffee can, which Bernard had buried under a lilac bush.)

"Not only will it be a real coffin," Bubs assured him.

"But it will be my uncle Walter's superdeluxe model," Nick interrupted. "It's bronze and lined with velvet."

The three were sitting on Bernard's fancy outdoor gym set in the Trauffmans' backyard by their big, fancy house. Like the house, the set was the biggest and fanciest in town. Bernard's father owned two supermarkets, so Bernard had the biggest and best of everything, from gym sets, to sneakers, to video games, to leather jackets. All of this was never enough for Bernard. He no sooner had the best of one thing than he wanted to have the best of something else.

"You'll be the only kid in town, maybe the only kid in the whole country, who ever had a funeral for his pet in a real funeral home," Bubs said. A wave of pleasure washed over Bernard's face and his lips curled into a greedy little smile.

Nick's voice was low and hypnotic. "You'll be the only one," he whispered, as Bernard's eyes glazed over. "Of course, if we use the casket, the ceremony will have to be in the chapel," Nick added.

"The chapel," Bernard repeated dreamily.

"Can't you picture it?" Nick whispered, as Bernard closed his eyes. "The music, the flowers, the candles, and your beloved Slim Jim laid out, not in some rusty old coffee can, but in Uncle Walter's top-of-the-line, velvet-lined casket. Imagine all that for only ten ninety-nine."

"Ten ninety-nine?" Bernard mumbled, as if in a trance. Nick and Bubs exchanged grins.

"It's a bargain price, for a funeral," Nick said. "You won't be sorry."

"I'll get the money out of my room," Bernard told them, jumping to the ground.

Nick and Bubs followed Bernard to the sprawling wood deck that wrapped around the back of the Trauffman house. Moose walked alone behind them, finally flopping down under the picnic table. Nick and Bubs sat and waited while Bernard ran into the house. Within minutes, he rushed back out with a handful of dollar bills. Nick couldn't take his eyes off the money, but Bernard was staring down at Moose's bright red shaggy tail sticking out from under the table.

"I still say that looks really weird," Bernard smirked.

"That's just because you've never seen anything like it before," Bubs said. "I guess I have the only dog around with a two-toned look." Nick rolled his eyes. He knew how annoyed Bernard got whenever someone had something he didn't, even it if was something as ridiculous as a dog's red tail.

"Let's start counting the money," Nick said hurriedly, seeing the scowl on Bernard's face.

"How do I know you aren't trying to trick me into loaning you this?" Bernard squinted suspiciously at the two boys.

"Bernard, I give you my word," Nick assured him. "My aunt and uncle are going away next weekend, and Slim's funeral is as good as done."

"Maybe I should wait and see," Bernard said, stuffing the dollar bills into his pockets. "You come through with your end of the bargain first, then I'll give you the money."

"See you at the funeral," Bubs muttered, as Bernard strode across the deck and into the house.

"You know," Bubs whispered, "if Bernard had a dog right now, I bet he'd run out and buy some Auburn Rinse. It must be killing him that old Moose is looking so good. Did you notice how his tail is brighter at the tip? It really is sort of two-toned."

Nick rolled his eyes. "Bubs, we didn't come here to show off Moose's two-toned tail! We came to get Bernard to give us the money."

"OK, OK, so all we have to do now is have the funeral," Bubs said, reaching down to stroke Moose.

"Right," Nick replied. "Besides, I always liked Slim Jim, even if his owner is a nerd."

"No reason to hold it against the snake," Bubs said, shaking his head.

*   *   *

" 'We at the Wiloby Funeral Home are here to serve all those in their time of need,' " Nick replied solemnly. "That's what Uncle Walter's ad says in the phone book."

"I don't think old Slim Jim could ask for more," Bubs grinned. "Why don't you come to my house so we can make plans while I wash off Moose's rinse?"

"I can't," Nick frowned. "I still have my chores to do. Uncle Walter expects me back home. Why don't you come to my house instead? We can talk while you help me. If there are two of us doing my chores, we can get everything done in no time."

Bubs sat thinking this over. "If you're dusting coffins, I'll come, but if you're doing yard work, count me out," he said. "I have enough of that to do at home."

"No, don't worry," Nick assured him. "Today is Saturday, so that means I start off with washing the hearse. When we're through we can have a hose fight and then we can wash off Moose." Bubs agreed, since having a hose fight sounded like fun. He had been Nick's best friend since kindergarten, and so being around hearses and coffins was almost as natural to Bubs as it was to Nick.

"I'll race you there," Nick called, springing to his feet. The two tore across the Trauffmans' lawn, with Moose close behind. When they reached the Wiloby Funeral Home, Nick saw that Uncle Walter had backed the long black hearse into the driveway. Beside it was a bucket filled with sponges, soap, rags, a toothbrush, and a can of car wax. Moose made his way under the hearse and curled up for a nap.

"OK, you can hang out there for a while, but once we're done with our work, we're turning the hose on you," Bubs called after him. "What's this for?" he asked. He bent down and pulled the toothbrush out of the bucket.

"Uncle Walter is so fussy about the hubcaps, he makes me use a toothbrush to clean out the dirt that gets in the cracks," Nick told him.

"Who looks at the hubcaps on a hearse?" Bubs wondered aloud.

Nick sighed. "Uncle Walter does. He spends lots of time trying to keep things clean. He's so fussy about his hearse, he won't let me clean the inside, which is fine with me."

Bubs began walking around the car.

"Wow, is that the fountain you were telling me about?" He pointed to the large blue cement fountain in the center of the front lawn. It had three levels, with a group of fish at the top. Their heads were flung back and their mouths were stretched open in an unnatural gape. Vincent, Uncle Walter's assistant, was on his hands and knees adjusting some pipe that was connected to the fountain's base.

"Vincent has been trying to get it to work for the last two days," Nick told Bubs. "The water is supposed to squirt out of the fishes' mouths. Uncle Walter and Vince drove all the way to Scranton to buy it. Let's see if he's got it working yet." When they reached the fountain, Vincent looked up and grinned.

"Hey, it's Heckle and Jeckle," he quipped. He always called them that. Vincent was a big burly man with ruddy red cheeks and black-and-gray curly hair. Unlike Uncle Walter, he liked to smile and laugh. Even though Vincent wasn't as serious as Uncle Walter would have liked, he was a good worker and had been with the family for years.

"You two are just in time for the grand unveiling," Vincent said.

"Have you got the fountain working yet?" Nick asked.

"Almost. We just need a couple of more

fittings. Your uncle went to the hardware store to get them. So what do you think? Pretty fancy for the likes of Wiloby, hey?"

"I never saw anything like it in town before." Bubs's voice was filled with admiration.

"The salesman said that it 'would add an air of distinction to the property,' " Vincent said, mimicking the salesman's snooty tone. "He said it would 'create a formal and elegant setting.' Well, that was all your uncle Walter had to hear. You know how he is always trying to improve the place."

"I think it's the only fountain in Wiloby," Nick added.

"Your uncle is hoping it stays that way. He's convinced that it will set the funeral home apart. His only worry is that old man Whipple, over at the Whipple Funeral Home in Ackermanville, will try and copy his idea. That's why he had me paint it." Vincent ran his hand over the sky-blue cement. "None of the fountains in the showroom were painted. The blue was your uncle's own idea."

"It looks like the color of a swimming pool," Bubs pointed out.

"As a matter of fact we used the same paint they use for painting swimming pools," Vincent said. "The paint is water-resistant and is kind of a restful blue. Always have to think restful in this business, you know," he added with a wink. Moose let out a bark from under the hearse, and Bubs went to check on him. Nick sat down on the grass.

"Vince," he began, "did you ever want to do something really different, something that would change your whole life?"

Vincent whistled as he began laying sod over the line of pipe. "Sure," he said. "Everyone wants to move forward some way or another. It's the way things work. We all have things we dream about."

"What if you had a dream that wasn't like everyone else's?" Nick continued.

Vincent scratched his head. "Oh, boy, those are the toughest kinds of dreams to have." He let out a loud sigh and reached for a length of pipe. "It reminds me of my cousin Frankie G. in New Jersey." (Vincent seemed to have hundreds of cousins, and they all lived in New Jersey.) "Now, Frankie's father wanted him to be a lawyer," Vincent went on. "The family had saved for years to send him to law school, but Frankie had other ideas."

"Didn't he want to be a lawyer?" Nick asked.

"No, Frankie wanted to tap-dance."

"So, did he become a tap dancer?" Nick asked.

"Well, he tried," Vincent said, breaking into a smile. "He traveled all over the country with a little dance troupe, but he finally had to give it up when the company folded."

"So, is he a lawyer now?" Nick asked.

"No, the last time I heard, he was running a Laundromat down in Atlantic City."

"Oh," Nick frowned, "so, his dream never came true."

"Well, not that one," Vincent chuckled, packing down another section of sod. "But the thing is, Frankie got to see the whole country, he met his wife out in California, and he had some really good times. You're going to have a lot of dreams, kiddo, and I can tell you right now, they probably won't all come true."

"So why bother having dreams at all?" Nick asked, pulling on a blade of grass.

"Because, if you don't try, you have no chance of anything happening," Vincent told him. "And sometimes, when you follow a dream, you can get lucky and find yourself in a better place, even if it isn't exactly where you had hoped to go."

Nick sat thinking this over. He thought about Vincent's cousin Frankie sitting in his Laundromat in Atlantic City. Vincent, as usual, seemed to be reading his mind.

"And you know what they have in Atlantic City, don't you?" Vincent said with a twinkle in his eye. Nick shook his head no.

"Taffy. Tons and tons of taffy. Why, Atlantic City is probably the taffy capital of the country, maybe of the world." Nick's eyes grew large. He had only tasted taffy once, when his aunt Jennifer had brought back a box of chocolate taffy from a vacation. He remembered how good it tasted.

"Do you think they have butterscotch taffy, too?" he asked.

"Do they?" Vincent whistled. "Kiddo, they have butterscotch, chocolate, vanilla, strawberry, peppermint, peanut butter . . . They have every flavor you've ever heard of and some you haven't."

Nick imagined Vincent's cousin Frankie in his little Laundromat, a stick of taffy hanging out of his mouth, tap-dancing from one washing machine to the next.

His daydream vanished, however, as Uncle Walter's car screeched into the driveway. Nick jumped up and hurried over to the hearse. Bubs was trying to brush Moose's teeth with the toothbrush.

"Well, here you are," Uncle Walter said, getting out of his car and slamming the door shut. He glanced at Bubs and then at Moose, who was sitting with his tail under the hearse and with his teeth clenching the toothbrush.

"You do realize that you have certain responsibilities . . ." Uncle Walter began, but Nick was fast to interrupt.

"I just went to get Bubs," he said. "He's going to help me. We can do a better job when there are two of us." Bubs smiled weakly and pulled the toothbrush out of Moose's mouth.

"Oh, all right, but you'd better do a good job," Uncle Walter said, walking over to the fountain.

Nick picked up the hose. "We'll get this done in no time, and then we'll work on Moose," he told Bubs. As Nick began to spray the hood of the hearse, he heard a familiar voice say, "My goodness, that's some fountain." Nick turned to see Mrs. Persetti standing next to Uncle Walter and Vincent.

"My mom!" gasped Bubs. "It's my mom! Quick, squirt Moose with the hose," he whispered, pulling Moose from under the hearse. As Bubs held onto his dog, Nick turned the hose on Moose's tail. The bright red dry tail turned into a bright red wet tail.

"She'll kill me!" Bubs moaned. Nick peeked from behind the hearse. The grown-ups were walking toward them. The boys would have to act fast.

"I'm dead! I'm dead!" Bubs whimpered.

Ducking down, Nick opened the hearse's back door and with Bubs's help, he shoved Moose through it. Seconds after he had shut the door, he heard Uncle Walter's voice.

"They were here a minute ago." Nick and Bubs sprang up and raced around to the front of the hearse.

"Good grief, Bubs," Mrs. Persetti gasped when Bubs almost ran into her, "how many times do I have to tell you to watch where you're going?" She brushed off her skirt and turned to Nick. "I was just introducing your uncle to your new neighbors," she said. Nick looked and saw a smiling man with a big nose and a thick mustache beneath it. Next to him stood a very pregnant woman. Nick glanced back at the hearse. He was glad that the inside windows were covered with curtains.

"I was showing a house down the street, and I noticed your car in the driveway," Mrs. Persetti said to the woman. "I'm sure you'll love the neighborhood."

Uncle Walter took a step toward Nick and placed his hand on his shoulder. "May I introduce my nephew, Nicholas, and his friend, Brian. (Uncle Walter always insisted on using proper names when he met new people.) "Boys, this is Mr. and Mrs. Rafferty. They're the people who bought the old Weston house. They'll be moving in tomorrow." Nick managed to smile weakly, and Bubs grinned beside him.

"Don't overdo it," Nick whispered in Bubs's ear. Bubs's grin faded instantly and his expression changed into a look of pain and surprise. Nick rolled his eyes. He knew that Bubs could never be a spy, since his face would always give him away.

"Is something wrong, Bubs?" Mrs. Persetti asked.

"Wrong? What could be wrong?" Bubs blinked nervously.

"What about kids?" Nick blurted, turning to Mrs. Rafferty. "Do you have any kids?"

"Don't worry, we've got plenty of those."

Mr. Rafferty laughed. "And more on the way."
He patted his wife's stomach. Everyone
smiled, everyone except Uncle Walter. He
looked too worried to smile. Nick knew how
much his uncle would hate having children
live so close to his funeral home. Children
were noisy, messy, and unpredictable.

"How many children do you have, exactly?"
Uncle Walter asked, his forehead beginning to
wrinkle.

"We've got four children," Mrs. Rafferty
told him. A little groan slipped out of Uncle
Walter's mouth.

"The kids are at their grandmother's today,
but if you stop by tomorrow, you can meet
them," Mr. Rafferty said, turning to Nick.

"I've got to stop back at the office," Mrs.
Persetti told Bubs, "and then I'm going to the
mall, if you two would like to come."

"Uh, no, thanks. We can't," Bubs sputtered.

"We still have some work to do," Nick told
her. "We've got to finish washing the hearse."

Mr. Rafferty grinned nervously. His wife's
smile seemed to sag.

"We've never lived next to a funeral home,"
Mr. Rafferty explained. "I guess it will take
some getting used to, but like I told the kids,

they won't have to worry about bothering the customers with their noise." He laughed loudly. Nick was about to laugh, too, until he heard Uncle Walter clearing his throat.

"Actually, Mr. Rafferty," Uncle Walter said, his voice crackling with anger, "my customers are the families of the deceased, and out of respect for their situation, I do require a quiet setting."

Just then a loud bark boomed from inside the hearse.

Chapter Four

The grown-ups stared at the hearse. Moose barked again, and Uncle Walter's lips trembled. Nick's stomach churned as he watched his uncle rush to the back of the hearse and open the door.

"Moose!" Mrs. Persetti cried as the dog bounded out, almost knocking Uncle Walter down. Leaping over the bucket of sponges, Moose raced to Mrs. Persetti and stood at her feet, wagging his bright red tail. Uncle Walter, whose face had turned almost as red as the tail, was about to say something when Mrs. Persetti cried, "His tail, what on earth happened to his . . ." She brought her hand to her head. Uncle Walter and the others stared first at Moose's tail and then at Mrs. Persetti's head

of hair. Vincent, meanwhile, had been working on the fountain. Once the new fitting was
secured, he walked over to the hose and
turned the water on.

"There she blows," he yelled. Everyone
watched as a rush of water shot from the blue
fishes' mouths and tumbled down into the
large blue bowls below.

"Wow!" Nick cried.

"Cool!" Bubs added. The two boys hoped
that the sight of the working fountain would be
so overwhelming, the grown-ups would forget
about Moose and the hearse. Unfortunately, at
the sound of the splashing water, Moose made
his way across the lawn, got up on his hind
legs, and lowered his head into the cool water
to take a drink.

The Raffertys and Vincent began to chuckle.
Mrs. Persetti, still clutching her hair, stood
frozen with embarrassment. Uncle Walter
wore a tight-lipped scowl. It wasn't until
Moose got down and lifted his leg, though,
that Uncle Walter actually spoke, if the
strained cry that came out of his mouth could
be called speaking.

Nick closed his eyes and pressed down on
the ball of his right foot. With his foot on the
gas, he imagined himself speeding down Route

22. It was a short trip, however, since the grown-ups sprang into action. Mrs. Persetti ordered Bubs and Moose into her car, while the Raffertys walked across the lawn to their new home. Nick could hear Mr. Rafferty laugh again as he passed the fountain. Uncle Walter growled some commands to Vincent, who hurriedly picked up his tools. Then Uncle Walter rushed over to the hearse.

"Nick, you get over here right now," Uncle Walter called. Nick winced at the sound of his uncle's voice.

"Look at the inside of this hearse," Uncle Walter fumed. "There are paw prints everywhere! What were you thinking of when you let that dog in here?" Nick squirmed, unable to answer, but his uncle didn't wait for a reply. "Don't you realize that this is my livelihood? What if that new loudmouthed neighbor decides to go and tell people about what happened today? Can you imagine what people will think? This is a very serious business. People expect a certain decorum and respectability. They don't expect to see dogs jumping out of a hearse!"

"I didn't mean for it to happen," Nick explained. "I was just trying to . . ."

"The only thing you'll try to do for the rest

of the day," Uncle Walter hissed, "is finish your work. And I'm telling you right now, there's going to be plenty of it. When you finish with the hearse, I want you to fold up all the chairs in the chapel and stack them by the door, so Vincent can take them over to the church. Then I want you to rake the stones out front. After that . . ." Nick groaned and closed his eyes as his uncle finished describing the worst possible Saturday any kid could imagine.

Later that day, after Nick had finished washing the hearse, he sat in the kitchen eating a turkey sandwich. Then he walked back out to the hallway and opened the door that led to the funeral home. He dragged himself down the stairs and entered the chapel. It was a large room filled with chairs. At the front was a long Oriental carpet that covered the trapdoor through which the caskets came up from the cellar. There was an orange button behind a curtain, which activated the hydraulic lift below. The casket was placed on the lift and then brought up to the chapel. Nick loved to push the button and listen to the lift hiss and hum. When Uncle Walter wasn't around, Nick would go into the cellar and place some of his army men on the lift, then run up to the chapel and push the button. Watching his guys come up on the lift was almost as good as being on it himself. Nick pushed the curtain aside now, and looked at the button longingly. He knew that today was not the day to push it.

He stared up at the two tall stained-glass windows on the far wall. The windows faced the backyard. Uncle Walter forbade any ball playing in the yard, since he didn't want a window to get broken. Nick imagined himself throwing a hardball straight at them. He imagined the delicious sound of a big crash, followed by a shower of brightly colored glass.

Next, Nick looked at the folding chairs. His heart sank at the sight of them. All seventy-five stood waiting for him. He would have to fold each one and carry it out of the chapel and into the hallway, so Vincent could load them into the truck. Uncle Walter loaned the chairs to the church for its monthly Bingo Bash. Nick hated folding chairs. It was almost as boring as raking stones, but at least the stones were outside.

Nick thought about how many chairs he would need for Slim Jim's funeral. He wouldn't need many—just one for Bernard, one for Bubs, and one for himself. After folding up a second chair, Nick sat down to take a break. He began to think about Slim Jim and what his life had been like.

"I bet it was great, being a snake," he mumbled to himself as he stretched out across two chairs with his hands behind his head. "If I were a snake," he said aloud, "I'd slip right out of here."

Nick closed his eyes and saw himself sliding through the grass and winding his way through the dirt, under the hedges, hiding in places where Uncle Walter could never find him. If I were a snake, he decided, I'd stay hidden all day and only come out at night when the moon was full and Uncle Walter was snoring in front of the TV.

Nick grinned as he imagined Uncle Walter snoring away in his easy chair with his head bent over a bowl of Cheezios. Uncle Walter loved Cheezios. Then Nick imagined himself slithering across the living room rug, up the back of Uncle Walter's easy chair and down into his bowl of Cheezios. He saw himself curling around the huge orange puffs. As a snake, he imagined that he could eat the whole bowl in just a few bites, while Uncle Walter dozed.

Nick closed his eyes and sniffed the air. He could almost smell a delicious heavy Cheezio scent. His mouth flopped open.

"If you keep your mouth open like that, you'll catch a fly." A little voice broke into his daydream. Nick's head snapped up. His little cousin Emily was standing by the door. She was chomping on a mouthful of bubble gum.

"My teacher, Miss Bently, talks about flies all the time when she sees somebody with his mouth open," Emily explained, before blowing a wobbly purple bubble.

"Name me one person that you know who ever swallowed a fly," said Nick. Emily sucked in her bubble and twisted one of her honey-colored curls around her finger.

"Well, somebody must have at one time," she said between chews, "or Miss Bently wouldn't have told us that."

Nick groaned. "You can't believe everything your teachers tell you, dummy."

"Miss Bently wouldn't lie," Emily declared, sitting down beside him. Miss Bently was Emily's favorite teacher.

"All right, so prove it," Nick demanded, scratching his head.

"How?" Emily asked.

"Sit there with your mouth open for a half an hour, and I'll bet you that not one fly will fly in."

"How much?" Emily asked. "How much will you bet?"

"Fifty cents," Nick told her.

Since Emily was only seven years old, there were certain things she didn't completely understand. She didn't know the real value of money. To her fifty cents seemed like a lot. Sitting with her mouth open for half an hour seemed worth doing for fifty cents.

"Should I start now?" Emily asked, taking the wad of gum out of her mouth and sticking it to the chair beside her.

"Sure, go ahead," Nick said. "Hey, did you hear about the new neighbors?" he asked. Emily sat, her head thrown back and her mouth wide open. She shook her head.

"They've got four kids," Nick said. "And they're expecting another one! Can you believe it?" Emily began making little grunting noises.

"Will you give up, Em? I can't have a conversation with you if you're going to sit there grunting. Haven't you noticed that there aren't any flies in here? And what would you do if one flew into your mouth, anyway?"

Emily squirmed. She looked at the gum that was getting dry on the chair. "Could I have the fifty cents anyway?" she asked, pulling the wad off the wood and popping it back into her mouth.

"No," Nick told her. "I'm saving all my money for something special." His little cousin's shoulders slumped. "Oh, OK, I'll give you twenty-five cents for trying."

"I'm glad there are a lot of kids moving in next door," Emily said, her face turning sunny. "Maybe there will be some girls my age."

"Well, I know somebody who's not glad at all," Nick said.

"Who?"

"Your father. You should have seen his face when he found out. You know how he hates kids."

"He doesn't hate me," Emily remarked. She blew another huge bubble.

"That's because you're his," Nick told her, "and you're a girl. If you were a boy and adopted like me, he'd hate you, too."

"Do you think Daddy hates you?" Emily asked, pulling the gum out of her mouth.

"Well, he sure doesn't love me," Nick said. "Not the way my real father would have. If my

dad were alive, we'd be doing all kinds of fun
things together. Uncle Walter is never happy
with anything I do. Do you know how many
times he made me wash the hearse today? Every time he looks at me, he thinks of more
work for me to do. My dad wouldn't have been
like that. If he were alive, we'd be taking trips
in his truck and playing baseball together.
Your dad hates baseball."

Emily frowned. "I know he hates baseball,"
she whispered, "but he couldn't hate you,
Nick. Nobody could hate you." Nick watched
as she opened her mouth and took out her wad
of gum. She silently handed it to him.

"Thanks, Em," Nick mumbled, putting the
gum into his mouth.

"I have to go to Becky's house now," Emily
said, walking to the door. With a worried look,
she turned and asked, "You won't feel bad anymore, will you, Nick? That gum is almost new.
I only chewed on it a couple of times."

"Naw, I don't feel too bad," Nick said. He
blew a good-sized bubble to prove it, then lay
back and closed his eyes.

Actually, I am feeling better, he thought.
He gave the gum one last chew before blowing
the biggest bubble he could. It was so enor-

mous, it covered most of his face. A warm satisfied feeling washed over him as he puffed a bit more air into his masterpiece. Yes, life was almost good again.

"Nick!" Uncle Walter's voice crackled like a firecracker going off beside him. Nick sucked in his bubble and jumped up as fast as he could. But the bubble broke all over his face, and in his haste, he tripped and fell to the floor.

"I don't know what I'm going to do with you," Uncle Walter grumbled, walking across the room. "You know that I don't allow any food or candy in the chapel. What if you should get gum on the carpet? Or worse, on the chairs. What would people think then? Would they want to use this funeral home again? No, I can bet you they wouldn't. Now, get up from there and go into the house and get rid of that gum. Then march back in here and finish folding these chairs."

Nick glared at Uncle Walter as he stomped past him to the yard. "What if I did get gum on the carpet?" Nick muttered to himself. "And what if someone did step on it? Would that be such a crime? And what if I did become a trucker someday, and I had my own rig?

Would I want to stick around here? No, I can bet you I wouldn't."

Nick walked up the stairs leading to the house. He could hear the whine of Uncle Walter's weeder-eater starting up, and his hands automatically went up to grab his imaginary steering wheel. After signaling, he made a sharp right turn, silently steering his rig through the kitchen and up the stairs to his bedroom. He flopped down on his bed, with his head at the foot, and stared up at the glossy calendar that hung on the wall. The calendar had been a birthday present from Vincent. It was a real truckers' calendar, with a picture of a different rig for each month of the year. This month's model was a candy apple red cab, with *Babe* spelled across the front grille in fancy silver letters.

Nick reached under his mattress and pulled out a wrinkled piece of paper. He lay back on the bed and held the paper up, reading the wobbly words written in his own hand:

"If I Could Have One Dream Come True It Would Be . . ." When his teacher had told the class that she was giving them a writing assignment last spring, Nick had moaned along with some of the other kids. He never seemed to have good ideas for writing, but when he saw the sentence Mrs. Riley had written on the board, he knew instantly what he would write about.

"My dream would be that my father and mother had never died," he wrote. "We would all live together in a nice house. My dad would take me for rides in his truck, and he would blow his horn whenever I asked him to." The paper fell onto Nick's stomach now, as he continued to recite aloud the words he had memorized by heart.

"My dad wouldn't care if my room were a mess, and he wouldn't care if there were weeds in our yard. The only thing we'd do in our yard would be to play baseball and wrestle. And when people saw us together they would always know that we were father and son."

Nick stared up at the truck on his calendar. He could see himself sitting beside his father who was behind the wheel in the cab. He could hear his father's friendly voice.

Nick was so lost in his daydream, he didn't notice the sudden silence as the weeder-eater died down.

"Nick!" Uncle Walter called from below his

window. Nick sprang up from the bed. He stuffed the paper under his mattress and headed for the door. Then he turned back and reached for a marker on his desk. As Uncle Walter's voice grew louder and louder, Nick jumped on his bed and circled Saturday, the thirty-first. Underneath it he wrote the letters *SJ'sF*. Then he threw the marker down, spit his gum across the room into one of his open dresser drawers, and rushed out the door.

Chapter Five

Nick woke up on Monday morning to the aroma of a freshly baked apple pie. "Good old Aunt Marge," he whispered out loud, his eyes still closed. Aunt Marge was happiest when she was dressed in her faded blue apron, a wooden spoon in hand, and with the scent of nutmeg and vanilla in the air. Nick liked to sit at the counter in the kitchen and watch his aunt's chubby fingers crimp a pie crust or roll out a circle of dough. Aunt Marge baked not only to make herself feel good, but to make others feel good, too.

"Poor Vincent," she would sigh, cracking some eggs into a bowl. "He got word that his mother is sick out in California, and he's so worried. We'll have to make him his favorite

rhubarb pie today. That will cheer him up."
And if it wasn't Vincent, it was Mr. Chapman,
the neighbor, or Cousin Peggy, or Uncle Joe.
There was always someone who needed cheer-
ing up.

And today, it's me, Nick thought. Aunt
Marge must know how many chores I've been
doing lately, and she feels sorry for me. Aunt
Marge knows how I feel. Nick hurried out of
bed. "And she knows how much I love apple
pie," he mumbled, racing down the stairs. But
when he reached the kitchen, Aunt Marge was
placing his apple pie in a picnic basket.

"Oh, good, Nick, I'm glad you're finally up."
Aunt Marge smiled as she handed him a bowl
and a spoon. He took his place beside Emily,
who was already gulping down her cereal.

"But what about my pie?" Nick asked. Aunt
Marge laughed.

"*Your* pie?" she asked.

"It's not yours, silly," Emily informed him,
"it's for the new neighbors."

"But why do they need an apple pie?" Nick
frowned, reaching for the box of cereal on the
table.

"It's a welcome pie, to welcome them to our
neighborhood," Aunt Marge explained. "Fin-

ish up your breakfast, and you and Emily can come with me when I take it over." Nick took his time. He was in no hurry to deliver *his pie* to the new neighbors. But the longer he sat at the table, the more Emily began to bother him. She tapped on the table and tugged on his arm.

"Come on, Nick, don't take so long," she whined. "Don't you want to meet the new kids?" Nick wasn't so sure about the new kids. He wasn't like Emily. He wasn't an optimist. Nick had learned that word last year from a book Mrs. Riley was reading aloud to the class. Mrs. Riley had explained that an optimist is someone who always thinks about the best that can happen, rather than the worst. Nick had instantly thought of Emily. She was definitely an optimist. He was not, he decided. It wasn't that he expected the worst, it was just that he was more cautious. He knew there were bad things that could happen as well as good, since his parents had died at the start of his life.

"Maybe I'll stay home and watch TV," Nick said casually.

"You can watch TV when we get back," Aunt Marge told him.

"If we hadn't spent the whole day at Aunt

Jen's yesterday," Emily complained, "we would have met the new neighbors, and I would be playing with their little girl right now."

"You'll have plenty of time to play with her, if there is a little girl your age," Aunt Marge said.

"Oh, they've got so many kids, they must have a girl my age," Emily announced, walking around the table. "I'm going to show her my room and my doll collection, and maybe we can become best friends," she said.

"Best friends? You haven't even met her yet!" Nick exclaimed. "What makes you so sure she'll even want to play with you?"

"Well, nobody wants to play with *you*, Icky Nicky," Emily answered with a smirk. Nick shrugged. Not only was Emily an optimist, she was a moody optimist. One moment she could be his best friend, and the next, his worst enemy.

"All I have to do is tell her what a little crybaby you are, and she'll think twice about coming over, much less being your best friend," Nick retorted. Aunt Marge looked at him and rolled her eyes.

"You don't know anything, Icky Nicky," Emily cried.

"All right, you two, that's enough," Aunt Marge said. "No one will want to come over here if you carry on like that." She went to the counter and picked up the picnic basket. "I hope they like apple pie," she said, walking to the door.

"Who wouldn't like apple pie?" Nick grumbled.

"Sticky Icky Nicky," Emily whispered, as she followed her mother. Nick was about to call her a name when Uncle Walter walked into the kitchen.

"What's going on?" he asked, tapping on the picnic basket.

"We're going over to welcome the new neighbors to the neighborhood," Aunt Marge said. "Why don't you come with us?"

Uncle Walter's face clouded. "No, thanks, Marge," he said. "I told you we already met on Saturday."

"Oh, but, Walter, this will be different," said Aunt Marge.

"No, you go over, I've got work to do," Uncle Walter said, turning and walking out of the room.

"Oh, good grief, Walter, the Raffertys aren't that bad," Aunt Marge called. Nick watched as Uncle Walter disappeared into the other

room. "He'll get over it," Aunt Marge whispered, shooing Nick and Emily out the back
door.

When they reached the Raffertys' yard, Nick
noticed that there were old toys everywhere.
Beat-up big wheels, a rusty wagon, sand toys,
broken dolls, plastic trucks, and army men
were spilling out of boxes on the big wide
porch and into the lawn. A bright yellow plastic baby pool was sitting in the middle of the
yard right where everyone could see it. Two
boys were bent over the pool. One was wearing a green snorkel and the other was wearing
a purple-and-black Batman mask. They were
in the middle of some underwater operation.
The surface of the water was cluttered with
floating army men and plastic boats.

Nick felt a wave of envy as he watched the
boys playing in their front yard. Uncle Walter
would never allow such a mess.

"Hello, there," Aunt Marge called. The boy
with the mask said "Hi." His brother took his
snorkel out of his mouth and smiled.

Aunt Marge introduced herself and Emily,
and then Nick heard her say, "This is my
nephew Nick."

"Hi, I'm Wallace," answered the boy with

the snorkel, "but everyone calls me Sam. And this is my brother William. Everybody calls him Willie." Willie nodded behind the Batman mask.

"You boys look to be about Nick's age," Aunt Marge said. "He'll be going into the fifth grade next year. What grade are you in, Sam?"

"I'll be going into fourth," Sam told them. "And so will Willie."

"Both of you?" Nick asked.

"Yup," said Sam. He lifted his brother's mask to reveal a face identical to his own. The same big brown eyes, the same dimples, the same red hair.

"We're twins," Willie declared.

"So we see." Aunt Marge laughed.

"Cool," Nick exclaimed. He had never seen identical twins before, and he couldn't take his eyes off them.

"Do you want to help us?" Willie asked. "We're reenacting the sinking of the *Titanic*."

Nick sat down beside them, while Aunt Marge and Emily went up to the house to meet the rest of the Raffertys. Sam handed Nick a block of wood and told him to pretend it was an iceberg. Nick rammed the block of wood into the side of the *Titanic*, and Sam tried to steady the sinking plastic craft. Willie made the passengers who had jumped ship cry out in distress. The courageous few who had dared to stay on board to rescue the women and children yelled words of encouragement. Great waves of water spilled out of the pool as army men went flying onto the grass. When the ship finally sank, the boys stirred the water with their arms and whooped loudly. The remaining army men were caught in the swirling current.

Nick was having such a good time, he was surprised to see his aunt and Emily come out of the house so quickly.

"Nick, we're going home now," Aunt Marge called. Nick noticed that she wasn't smiling as much as she had been earlier. Emily wasn't smiling at all.

"Why don't you stay and play?" the twins suggested.

"OK, I'll see if I can," replied Nick. "Aunt Marge," he called, "would it be all right if I stayed for a while?" Aunt Marge hesitated and then finally nodded.

Nick spent the rest of the morning helping the two boys sink one ship after another. They created hurricanes, tornadoes, and volcanoes.

Willie ran into the house for some supplies for the volcano while Nick and Sam discussed their favorite foods.

"My favorite is pickles," said Sam, "and Willie's favorite is strawberry ice cream. He could eat a whole gallon if we let him." Nick told him that his favorite food was Cheezios, followed by olives, but only the black ones. The two sat talking about food for a while longer, and then they began to discuss pets. Nick told Sam all about Bubs and Moose and Moose's two-toned tail.

"That sounds cool," Sam said. "My older sister Carrie is always dying her bangs. They've been pink, orange, blue, and purple. Almost every color in the rainbow, except green. She looks really gross."

"Do you have any younger sisters?" Nick asked, thinking of Emily.

"Um, Annie. She's only seven. Annie's OK, but sometimes she gets on my nerves."

"I know how that is," Nick said, shaking his head. Nick wondered why Annie and Emily weren't playing together. Meanwhile, Willie came out of the house with a box of baking soda and a bottle of vinegar. The three boys searched the yard for the best location to set up their volcano. They finally decided to place it on an old anthill by the side of the house.

Willie poured the baking soda onto the hill and asked Nick about his parents. "Are they divorced or something? Is that why you live with your aunt and uncle?"

"No, my parents are dead," Nick told him. The twins fell silent. There were a lot of kids who had divorced parents, but dead parents was a category of experience all by itself. The twins looked at Nick with newfound respect. Willie's eyes grew big.

"Were they murdered or something?" he whispered.

Nick shook his head.

"Willie, you watch too much TV," said Sam.

"They died in a car crash when I was just a baby," Nick told them. "I've lived with Aunt Marge and Uncle Walter ever since."

"So what's it like to live in a funeral home?" Sam asked.

"Do you get to see a lot of dead bodies?" added Willie.

"Naw, my uncle has these different rooms in the funeral home. One is the embalming room. That's where the bodies are. But he keeps it locked."

"Are there any bodies in there now?" asked Willie, inching closer to his twin.

"No, but there are caskets," Nick whispered.

"You mean, like coffins?" Willie croaked.

"Um, we've got all kinds," Nick said. "They're in the casket room, and that room isn't locked. It's right under the chapel and the trapdoor."

"Oooo . . ." The twins shivered. As their eyes grew bigger and bigger, Nick began to see his life at the Wiloby Funeral Home in a new light. It no longer seemed boring and dull, but suddenly interesting and almost exotic.

"Tell us more," Willie begged. Nick paused, savoring the fact his audience was hanging on his every word. He lowered his eyelids, hoping to look more mysterious. Then he went on to describe the Wiloby Funeral Home's caskets in detail.

Chapter Six

"I thought this was supposed to be a secret funeral," Bubs commented on Tuesday, after Nick said he was thinking of inviting the Rafferty twins to Slim Jim's service. He and Nick were sitting on Nick's bed, looking through comic books. Bubs was going to spend the night.

"It still is a secret," Nick answered. "I just thought it would be nice if Slim Jim had a few more people there."

"Nice for Slim Jim?" Bubs's eyebrows shot up. "I doubt old Slim will be taking a body count, since he *is* the body, isn't he? Don't you think it's kind of dangerous asking these new kids? What if they tell their parents, and your uncle finds out?"

"They won't tell anyone," Nick assured him. "I'll have them swear before I invite them. Don't worry, I trust them. I told them all about you and Moose."

Moose let out a loud sigh from under the bed. Ever since he'd discovered the fountain, a number of other dogs had begun making daily pilgrimages to the Wiloby Funeral Home fountain, first for a little refreshment, then for a little relief.

Just that morning, Uncle Walter had been having his breakfast when he looked out the window and spotted the first offender of the day. It was Thor, the Sylvestris' frisky German shepherd puppy that lived around the block. Before Uncle Walter could race down the porch steps and out into the yard, Mrs. Car-nicelli's old black poodle, Banjo, had joined the puppy at the fountain. Uncle Walter squirted both of them with the hose and chased them down the block with a broom. It was then that he decided to make a new "dog rule." No dogs would be allowed to stay on the property unless they were on a leash.

"But Bubs doesn't have a leash for Moose," Nick had protested.

"Then I'm afraid we won't be seeing much

of Mr. Moose around here," Uncle Walter replied. Nick and Bubs found an old clothesline rope in the Persettis' garage and hooked it to Moose's collar. Now Moose let out another depressed sigh from under the bed.

"I don't think he likes the clothesline," Bubs whispered. "He's never had to be on a leash before. I think it makes him feel stupid." Nick put down his comic book and walked over to the window. He looked out and watched Vincent planting flowers in a ring around the fountain. Uncle Walter was standing beside him. Nick pressed his nose to the screen. He could hear Vincent's deep voice.

"I don't know about these flowers," Vincent was saying. "Maybe if they had thorns on them, they would keep away dogs, but I don't see how these skimpy little things are going to do anything." He shook his head, then dug another hole with his trowel.

"They're marigolds, Vincent," Uncle Walter explained in a serious, all-knowing tone. "And marigolds have an odor that is disagreeable to many insects."

"That's all well and good," Vincent chuckled, "but we're not talking about mosquitoes sprinkling on your fountain. What we've got here is a canine problem."

Nick giggled.

"I know that, Vincent," Uncle Walter snapped, "but my hope is that the marigolds will also be disagreeable to the dogs. The woman at the store thought they might. I picked up this powder, too. It's supposed to keep dogs away. When you've finished planting the marigolds, sprinkle a ring of this around them. That should be the end of our problem."

"If you say so," Vincent muttered.

"Will you watch what you're doing?" Uncle Walter ordered. "You're going out of the circle with that one." He pointed to the marigold that Vincent had just planted. Nick moved away from the window. He hated to hear his uncle snap at Vincent.

"Supper's ready," Aunt Marge called from the kitchen. Nick and Bubs raced down the stairs and almost toppled over one another as they jumped off the last step.

"Oh, boys, go and call Emily, will you?" Aunt Marge asked. "I think she's playing in the backyard."

"Sure, Aunt Marge," Nick replied. He and Bubs went outside to look for her. The backyard was empty, and the boys were about to return to the kitchen when they heard voices.

Nick walked over to the hedge that separated the Hadleys' yard from the Raffertys'. He saw a freckled-faced little girl who had the same dimples as Sam and Willie Rafferty. Nick guessed that she was their sister Annie. She was standing beside two other girls. Nick recognized one of them from Emily's class. Emily was standing alone, away from the others.

"This doll's name is Amy and this one is Firefly," Emily said.

"That's a dumb name. Why call her Firefly?" Annie Rafferty asked.

"Because she was lost in the woods and some fairies found her and gave her that name," Emily explained. Nick groaned. He knew that Emily changed the names of her dolls every time she made up a new story about them.

"If you want to come over, I'll show you my other dolls. I've got a lot more up in my room. We can all play there," Emily suggested.

"My mother says that she doesn't want me to play in a funeral home," Annie Rafferty sniffed.

"But I don't play in the funeral home," Emily protested. "Our house is over the funeral home."

"Her house must be creepy if it's over a

funeral home," one of the other girls taunted.

"It is not," Emily insisted. Her cheeks flushed a deep red. "I'm going to tell my mom what you said."

"Go ahead," said Annie Rafferty. "My mom says that your mom and dad must be weird to want to hang around dead bodies all the time. You're like the Addams family."

Emily bit down on her lip. "We are not. You don't even know us," she cried. Then she picked up her box of dolls and ran across the yard. Laughing, the girls turned and walked back to the Raffertys' porch. Nick started to take a step toward them, but Bubs reached out and stopped him.

"They're just a couple of dumb girls," Bubs said.

"I know, but I feel bad for Emily," said Nick between clenched teeth. "I'm going over there and make them take it back."

"Nick, will you hurry inside? The spaghetti is getting cold," Aunt Marge's voice called from the kitchen. "And I have a nice blueberry cobbler for dessert." Reluctantly Nick turned around and headed for the house. Bubs followed.

Both boys sat down at the long kitchen table, and Aunt Marge dished out the spaghetti. Uncle Walter was sitting at the head of the table. He took a deep breath. Besides the smell of homemade spaghetti sauce, the kitchen was filled with a cinnamon blueberry aroma.

"I have a little something for you two," Uncle Walter said, reaching over to the counter beside the table. He handed Bubs a bag. Nick watched as Bubs reached into the bag and pulled out a red leather leash.

"Gee, thanks!" Bubs exclaimed.

"I thought it would hold up better than that old clothesline rope," Uncle Walter said, smiling.

"It sure will. And Moose will look great on the end of this. Look, Nick, it even has a tag for his name."

"Everyone in the neighborhood knows his name is Moose," Nick commented. "The clothesline rope worked just as well."

"Nick, your uncle made a special trip to the pet shop to pick that up," Aunt Marge said. "I think you owe him a thank-you, at least."

"I didn't ask him to buy the leash," Nick protested.

Aunt Marge shook her head. "That's not the point, Nick . . ."

"It's OK, Marge," Uncle Walter said, raising his hands from the table and looking away. "So where is Emily?" he asked, changing the subject. The boys fiddled with their spaghetti. Everyone knew that Emily loved blueberries, and blueberry cobbler was her favorite dessert.

"Nick, please go and call her again," Aunt Marge said.

"I don't think she's too hungry," Nick replied.

"Not hungry for blueberry cobbler? Since when has Emily ever passed up blueberry cobbler?" Uncle Walter asked. Nick picked up his fork and put it down again. He knew he would have to tell them.

"Since the new Rafferty girl and a couple of other kids made fun of her for living in a funeral home," he blurted.

"Oh, I was afraid of that," Aunt Marge said, putting down the spoon in her hand. "Emily really had her heart set on making friends with that little girl, but it seems Mrs. Rafferty is uncomfortable with the idea of her children playing over here." Nick could see the hurt look in his aunt's eyes.

"I don't see why," Bubs said.

"Because we run a funeral home," whispered Uncle Walter, lowering his eyes. "And because some people think it's a strange profession. So strange that they won't let their children play with mine. Poor Emily. I'll go see how she is." He stood up and walked out of the kitchen.

"I'm not going to play with those stuck-up Rafferty kids anymore," Nick said, jabbing at a meatball.

"Now, Nick." Aunt Marge shook her head. "You said you had a good time with Sam and Willie the other day. I don't want you to lose friends on account of what's going on with Emily. Sam and Willie seem like nice boys to me. Don't worry, we'll work this all out." She turned toward the stairs. "Start your dinner now. Your uncle and I will be right back."

Nick and Bubs sat at the table, staring at their spaghetti in silence. Bubs was the first to speak.

"It's too bad your uncle wasn't a dentist. Nobody makes fun of my dad for being a dentist, and we get tons of free toothpaste."

Nick tried to smile, but somehow the thought of tons of free toothpaste didn't make him feel any better.

Chapter Seven

On Wednesday morning, Nick and Bubs worked at pulling out the weeds that had poked through the white stones surrounding the Wiloby Funeral Home sign. Nick hated pulling weeds even more than folding chairs.

"If you two do a good job and get all these weeds pulled, I'll take you to the mall for a hamburger this afternoon," Uncle Walter offered, as he surveyed their work.

Nick shrugged. "We don't want to go to the mall today," he muttered.

"Not even if we stop at the video arcade?" asked Uncle Walter. Bubs let out a little squeak of pleasure, but Nick continued to shrug.

"No, we don't want to go to the arcade.

We've got some other stuff we'd rather do," he said.

Uncle Walter frowned. "Well, if you change your minds, let me know," he said. Then he walked into the garage.

"What other stuff do we have to do?" Bubs asked. "What could be better than going to the video arcade?"

"I just don't feel like going, all right?" Nick snapped.

"Why? Because it was your uncle's idea? If your aunt Marge had offered to take us, you would have gone, wouldn't you?"

"Maybe, I don't know," Nick mumbled.

"Your uncle isn't as bad as you think, Nick. My dad never takes me to the arcade. At least your uncle does that."

"But he's *not* my dad. He's my uncle. And that makes it different. If my dad were alive, we'd be going to the arcade all the time, and it would be fun, not like when Uncle Walter takes me."

"How do you know?" Bubs asked. "I mean, how do you know that you'd have a better time with your dad? If he died when you were just a baby, you never really knew what he was like. He could have been more like your uncle than you think."

Nick groaned as he pulled another weed. "No one is like Uncle Walter, believe me. You don't know, because you don't have to live with him. With Uncle Walter, everything has to be perfect. Take these weeds, for example. Look how pretty these flowers are and yet he hates them." Nick held up a handful of bright yellow dandelions.

"They are pretty, almost as pretty as the ones he planted around the fountain," Bubs admitted.

"When I grow up, I'm going to let the weeds grow and get rid of the other stuff," Nick decided. "Of course, I'll be on the road a lot, driving my truck, so my place will look like a jungle when I get back. My grass will be so high, you won't be able to see my house. Won't that be cool?"

"Um," Bubs nodded. "If your grass grows to be twelve feet high, imagine all the neat animals that could live in it."

"Yeah, and I'll get a great big fountain, twice as big as Uncle Walter's, and I'll put a huge sign next to it that says,

DOGS ONLY
NO PEOPLE ALLOWED
UNLESS ON A LEASH

Both boys laughed. Then Nick began to day-dream about his life as a long-distance trucker.

"Maybe you could come with me on some of my trips," he mused. "I want to drive all around the country, the way my dad did, hauling all kinds of things. For my first trip, I'll go to someplace like Florida. I'll pick up a load of alligators to bring to the zoo in Philadelphia. You can come with me and we'll stop off at Disney World or Sea World."

"I've always wanted to go to Disney World," Bubs said, "but I don't know if I want to be fooling around with any alligators. Couldn't you carry something with less teeth, like oranges or something?"

"Bubs, a long-distance trucker is expected to take risks," Nick told him. "That's what the job is all about. Truckers have to be willing to carry any kind of cargo, even toxic waste and radioactive stuff. That's what makes the job so exciting."

"I'd still rather have oranges than alligators," Bubs insisted. "Can't we start out with oranges first?"

"OK, we'll start off with a load of oranges and work our way up to the more exciting stuff."

"Instead of oranges, how about a truckload of peanuts?" Bubs suggested. "I love peanuts. I could eat a hundred peanuts and never get sick of them."

"Sure, we can haul whatever we like." Nick pulled another weed. "I can just picture it, living on the road, traveling wherever we want to go, and getting paid for it, besides. I can't wait to get *The Truckers' Road Atlas*. I'll be able to start mapping out trips and reading about all the different highways."

"Before you get the atlas, you'll have to give Slim his funeral," Bubs reminded him.

"That's as good as done," Nick said, standing up and throwing a weed clump that hit Bubs in the arm. Bubs jumped to his feet and took a step backward. Then he threw a clump of weeds at Nick, hitting him on the side of the head.

"Yuck!" Nick cried, shaking the dirt out of his hair.

"Ooo, direct hit!" Bubs laughed. "Hey, Nick, are you still inviting those Rafferty kids after what happened with Emily?"

Nick shook his head. "No way. I don't want to have anything to do with that family. As far as I'm concerned, if you're a Rafferty, you're an enemy." He picked up another weed clod.

"Right," Bubs announced loyally. "Then they're my enemies, too."

"I knew I could count on you, Bubs." Nick threw a clod that whizzed below Bubs's knee. Soon there were weed clumps flying back and forth.

"You never throw high enough," Bubs yelled.

"Oh yeah? Well check this out!" Nick shouted. He reached down to pick up the biggest clod yet. He arched his arm back as far as he could. Bubs dove to get out of the line of attack. Nick released his arm and the giant weed clod went sailing over Bubs's head and across the lawn. It came down over Uncle Walter's fountain, landing on the head of one of the blue fishes.

Bubs howled with laughter. "You gave that fish hair!" It was true, the grassy-looking clump did look a lot like hair. Nick was laughing, too, until he heard the side door squeak.

"It's Uncle Walter!" he cried. "Quick, the hideout." Uncle Walter came around the corner, and Nick and Bubs dove through the bushes and raced to Nick's hideout under the old hemlock tree. The green needles of the tree's branches offered a cool dark umbrella of privacy.

Nick crouched, trying to catch his breath, while Uncle Walter walked into the garage. "Nick," he called.

"He hasn't seen the hairy fish yet," Nick whispered to Bubs.

"How do you know?" Bubs whispered back.

"I can tell by the sound of his voice," Nick explained. "When he gets supercrabby, his voice changes. When he sees that fish, it'll sound like this." But before he could imitate Uncle Walter, the sound of a truck's air horn blasted through the air.

Nick stuck his head out between the hemlock branches. An orange tractor trailer-cab was pulling into the Raffertys' driveway. It was the cab of an eighteen-wheeler, a real eighteen-wheeler! Nick couldn't believe his eyes. He jumped out of the hideout and wedged himself between the hedges to get a better view.

"Wow, what a beauty," he whispered. He stared at its flawless orange finish and shiny steel grille. The words *Peach Blossom* were spelled out across the front of the hood. Two shimmering exhaust pipes rose up like rocket boosters on either side of the back window. Nick took a step into the Raffertys' yard. He read the words that were spelled out in bold black letters on the driver's door:

A.T. TRUCKING
MANVILLE, NEW JERSEY

It was the first big rig that Nick had ever seen up close, except for those on the highway, and they were always moving. But this was idling before him, full of shimmering steel, powerful rubber, and the glory of the open road. When the driver's door opened, Nick half expected to see his father jump out, the truck was so like the trucks in his daydreams. He couldn't have been more surprised to see Mr. Rafferty.

"Hi, Dad," Sam and Willie Rafferty called out from behind a table they had set up on the sidewalk. There was a plastic pitcher of lemonade in front of them, and beside it a big paper sign in the shape of a lemon. The words LEMONADE 25¢ A GLASS were written on it.

"That's just what I need," Mr. Rafferty said. "I'll take two glasses." Sam poured the lemonade, and Willie took the money and put it in a jar.

"That lemonade looks good," Bubs whispered.

"How about a ride, Dad?" the twins begged. Mr. Rafferty drank his lemonade and put down the glasses.

"It'll have to be a short one," he said, rubbing his back. "I just drove six hours straight through."

"Just down the street, please, Dad?" they whined.

"Well, OK, but let me run into the house for a pit stop first. I'll be back in five minutes, so be ready."

"I don't believe it," Nick whispered. "Their father is a trucker. And they never even told me!"

"They probably don't think it's that big a deal," Bubs said. "Not everyone thinks that truck driving is so great."

"It's one of the best jobs there is!" Nick said. Just then Sam Rafferty turned around and caught sight of Nick and Bubs. He waved and ran over to them.

"Hi, Nick, how's it going?" Sam asked.

"OK," Nick answered, shifting nervously from foot to foot.

"I bet you're the Bubs," Sam said, grinning

at Bubs. "Nick told me all about you and your dog Moose. How'd you like to have a glass of lemonade, for free?" Bubs started to smile, but rolled his eyes in Nick's direction to check on Nick's reaction. Nick did not look happy.

"We have to go," Nick said.

"Hey, wait," Willie called out, "why don't you come for a ride in our dad's truck?"

Nick stared at them. He hated the way Annie Rafferty had hurt Emily. He hated the way Mrs. Rafferty's words had made Aunt Marge look so sad. He thought he might even hate Sam and Willie just because they were Raffertys. But he positively loved the idea of taking a ride in their father's truck.

"What's the matter?" Sam asked. "Don't you want to come?"

"Naw, we've got other stuff to do in my secret hideout," Nick answered coolly. "Your father's truck is dumb-looking. Who would want to ride in a truck called *Peach Blossom,* anyway?" Sam and Willie glared at him. "Come on, Bubs, we've got some important stuff to do." Bubs looked longingly at the lemonade stand, then followed Nick home through the hedges.

Chapter Eight

"So what important stuff do we have to do this time?" Bubs asked. They were back in Nick's hideout.

"How should I know?" Nick said, sinking to the ground. "I had to say something, and it was the only thing I could think of."

"It sounded good." Bubs tried to make him feel better. "And the bit about riding in a dumb truck called *Peach Blossom*, that sounded great." Nick closed his eyes and lay down on the needle-covered ground.

"Did you see how surprised they looked when I said it?" he asked.

"Uh-huh," Bubs agreed. "I guess they didn't know they were the enemy."

"Well, they sure do now." Nick was lost in

thought, thinking about what the Rafferty twins *didn't* know. They didn't know that he really *did love* the look of their father's truck, with its smooth orange-apricoty paint job and its fancy black lettering. And that he would give anything to have his own father alive, taking him for rides with him in a truck like the *Peach Blossom.* He even loved the name *Peach Blossom,* the way it rolled so easily off his tongue.

"Why is it that some people have all the luck?" Nick asked.

"I don't know," Bubs said, trying to coax an ant onto his index finger. "My mom says that some people are just born under a lucky star."

"It must have been pitch-black on the night I was born," Nick moaned, "without a star in the sky."

"You don't have it so bad," Bubs said, staring down at the ant. "Your uncle offered to take you to the arcade. And at least you don't have to take trumpet lessons."

"Huh?" Nick looked confused.

"Yeah, my dad found his old trumpet in the attic last week, and now he wants me to take lessons. At least your uncle isn't making you take trumpet lessons."

"Nick," Uncle Walter called suddenly, his

voice bristling with crabbiness. "Nick, where are you?"

"Like I said, pitch-black," Nick groaned, getting to his feet. He and Bubs crawled out from under the tree. They could see Uncle Walter frowning. He was surveying the weeds that were strewn all over the lawn. Both boys stole a glance at the fountain. The clump of weeds was still firmly planted on the fish's head, although Uncle Walter hadn't noticed it.

"We'll get the ladder out of the garage and pull the weeds off the fish after Uncle Walter goes back inside," Nick whispered to Bubs.

"Nick, you've got to learn to be more responsible," Uncle Walter called. "When you're given a job, you're to do it, and do it right. This is not where the weeds are to go," he snapped, pointing to a clump of weeds lying in the grass. With eyes lowered and finger outstretched, he proceeded to march around the yard, pointing to one clump after another. Nick and Bubs followed closely behind with the wheelbarrow, stealing anxious glances at the fountain every now and then.

Nick breathed easier when Uncle Walter finally headed back to the house. But the sound of a truck's horn stopped him in his tracks. Nick's shoulders stiffened as the mighty *Peach*

Blossom pulled up to the curb. Uncle Walter smiled a tight little smile.

"Hey, Walter, looks like your blue fish are growing some green hair," Mr. Rafferty called. Uncle Walter glanced at the fountain. His eyes almost popped out of his head.

"Not a star in the sky," Nick mumbled, as Mr. Rafferty's laughter was drowned out by the roar of the truck's engine. Nick watched as the *Peach Blossom* pulled away from the curb. Then he dragged himself over to the fountain.

"This is the last straw," Uncle Walter fumed. "I can't even give you the simplest job without you making a mess of things. How many times do I have to say it? This is a funeral home and people expect order and tidiness, not weeds thrown all over the place. Now get this mess picked up before I really lose my temper."

Later that afternoon, after all the chores were *responsibly* done, Nick and Bubs decided to have a picnic lunch in the secret hide-out. It was a hot day, and the hemlock tree next to the hedge offered the only cool spot in the yard. Nick filled an old bookbag with some things he thought they could use—paper, markers, colored pencils, a box of baseball cards, a magnet, two paper clips, some string, three comic books, a shoebox full of stickers, and a game of Chinese checkers. Nick carried the bookbag and Bubs carried their lunch. Aunt Marge had packed juice, sandwiches, grapes, and homemade brownies. Once in the privacy of the hideout, Bubs unwrapped the brownies.

"You're luckier than you think, Nick," he said, munching on the rich chocolaty dessert. "My mom never makes brownies like this. She's always busy working, and when she does come home, she's too tired to bake."

"Aunt Marge does bake a lot," Nick agreed, stuffing a brownie into his mouth. They continued to eat and talk about all the good things Aunt Marge baked. By the time they were finished talking, the brownies were all gone.

"I guess we should eat the sandwiches now," Nick said, offering a ham sandwich to Bubs. They were halfway through their sandwiches when they heard Vincent's van pull into the driveway. Nick poked his head through the branches to have a look.

"Vincent's back from Crimms's," he whispered.

"What's Crimms's?" Bubs asked.

"Crimms's Casket Company," Nick replied. "It's where Uncle Walter buys a lot of his caskets. I heard him tell Aunt Marge that he was sending Vincent to pick up two new ones. One is called the Embassy, and it's made of bronze. They're the most expensive."

"Did he have someone in mind?" Bubs asked. "You know, to go into the Embassy. I mean, did someone just die?"

"No," Nick said, taking another bite of his sandwich, "Uncle Walter likes to keep different models in the showroom. Come on, let's go check it out." He and Bubs stepped out from under the tree branches. They found Vincent standing at the back of the van.

"Hey, Heckle and Jeckle," said Vincent.

"Hi, Vince," the boys called, looking into the van.

"There she is," Vincent said. "The Embassy, top of the line, as they say." The casket didn't look all that different from the other caskets Nick had seen in the showroom. It was long and dark brown and wrapped in plastic.

Vincent sat down on the bench beside the garage and worked on taking a stone out of his shoe.

"Is that the kind of casket you want to be buried in when you die?" Bubs asked Vincent.

"Naw," Vincent said, shaking the stone out of his shoe, "I don't need anything that fancy.

That casket there will be for some rich big-wig, maybe a judge or a mayor or somebody who has been used to lots of frills. Me, I'm a simple workingman. Plan on going out as simple as I can." He put his foot back into his shoe. "Where's your uncle?" he asked, looking at Nick.

"He was sitting in front of the air conditioner, eating lunch, last time I saw him," Nick replied.

Vincent wiped the sweat from his forehead. "Um, sure is a hot one today," he said.

"What's the hottest day you can remember, Vince? The hottest day of your life," Nick said, sitting on the grass beside the bench. Vincent smiled faintly.

"Well, let me see," Vincent said, rubbing his chin. His voice turned serious. "That would be the summer of fifty-five. I was a little sprout, shorter than either of you, and I was staying at my cousin Johnny's place on the Jersey shore. It was so hot that summer that the ocean dried up."

"No way," Bubs smirked. He had sat down beside Nick. "That can't happen."

"What can't?" Vincent asked, a look of surprise on his face.

"The ocean," Bubs said. "It never dries up."

"Oh, never say never," Vincent chuckled. "You'd be surprised at the things that happen that are never supposed to happen."

"So, what happened?" Nick asked. Vincent looked confused.

"When the ocean dried up," Nick reminded him.

"Oh, that was a sight! Johnny and I were standing on the beach, and as far as we could see, there were boats everywhere, stranded this way and that."

"What about the fish?" Bubs asked. "What happened to all of them?"

Vincent smiled. "That's the two-million-dollar question. What happened to the fish? They had all disappeared, but where to?"

"I don't know, you're telling the story," Bubs protested. "You should know where they all went."

"No, Bubs," Nick corrected him, "that's not how we do it. Vince starts out telling the story, and then we have to finish it. Here, I'll show you." He looked up at Vincent.

"Did an alien ship come from another planet and suck them all up?" he asked. Vincent shook his head no.

"How about one monster whale that opened

his mouth so wide, all the fish got eaten up?" Nick continued.

"That would have had to have been a big, big whale," Vincent said, still shaking his head. "I don't think they come that big."

"OK, OK, I got it this time," Nick said. "There was this little fishing boat . . ."

"You're on to something there," Vincent grinned.

"Right," Nick said. "And this little fishing boat had one little old man in it. He had one fishing line and one little worm on the end of his line."

"But what kind of worm was it?" Vincent asked. Bubs and Nick sat thinking.

"A magic worm!" Nick suddenly cried out.

"Exactly!" Vincent replied.

"And that one little worm pulled in every fish in the sealess sea," Nick continued.

"Even the whales and the sharks?" Bubs asked.

"Even the whales and sharks." Nick nodded. "And that little old man sold all those fish to a market, and he became a million billion trillionaire."

"That's just what happened," Vincent said. "And he retired to Miami, so he could watch the sun set over the ocean and eat as many clams as he wanted. The only problem was, there was no more ocean for the sun to set over and without an ocean there could be no clams."

"So, did he get another little fishing boat and go out with another magic worm that would bring all the fish back?" Bubs asked. But Vincent sat shaking his head.

"No, he moved to Arizona," Vincent told him, "where he could watch the sun set over the desert and where he acquired a taste for tacos." Nick smiled as the story ended. Bubs looked confused.

"What about the ocean?" he demanded. "How did the water come back?"

"That's another story," Vincent told him. "Maybe the next time it's raining, you should ask me about the day it started raining and wouldn't stop. Then I'll tell you about the ocean filling back up." He stood and winked at Nick. "Right now, I'd better get back to work."

"Don't you love Vincent?" Nick asked, after he and Bubs had returned to the hideout to finish their lunch.

"Yeah, he's pretty neat," Bubs agreed. "Except, I'd still like to know how the ocean filled back up." As he and Nick sat talking, they heard some noises coming from the Raffertys' front yard.

"They're setting up their lemonade stand again," Bubs whispered, taking a peek.

"So let them," Nick replied. He started to lay out the Chinese-checker board. "We've got better stuff to do than sell lemonade." Soon the two boys were lost in the game. Their concentration was broken, however, by the sound of twigs crackling nearby. Nick froze as he heard Willie Rafferty say, "Wow, look, it's a coffin!"

"He's really creepy-looking, isn't he?" Sam Rafferty whispered back. The two had snuck between the hedges to get a better view of Vincent unloading the van. They were almost on top of the hemlock hideout. Nick and Bubs didn't dare move.

"At first I thought Nick was an OK kid," Willie whispered.

"Well, he's not," Sam replied. "Not after what he said about Dad's truck. He must be as creepy as the rest of them. Look at that big guy wheeling the coffin. He looks like he could be in a monster movie." Nick clenched his fists.

"Maybe he's part monster," Willie suggested. "A kind of Frankenstein monster that Nick's uncle made from all the dead bodies he gets." Nick felt as if someone had slapped him in the face. He squinted, trying not to cry. How could they talk about Vincent that way?

"Look out, he's coming this way," Willie Rafferty cried, running back to the lemonade stand. Nick sprang up and looked through the branches.

"Oh, no," he whispered as he watched Vincent making his way over to the Raffertys' front yard.

"Please, go back, please, go back," Nick muttered under his breath. Then he heard Vincent say, "Looks like some great lemonade. I'll take one glass."

Chapter Nine

Willie's hands shook when he poured Vincent a glass of lemonade. Sam trembled as he reached out to take Vincent's twenty-five cents.

"They look as if they've seen a ghost," Bubs whispered from inside the hideout. "It's kind of funny, the way they're so afraid of Vincent."

"Didn't you hear what they called him, Bubs?" Nick said. "They said he was creepy-looking. They called him a monster. That's not funny."

"Well, I only meant . . ." But before Bubs could finish his sentence, the two boys heard Vincent calling to Mr. Rafferty. Vincent walked over to where he was working in the garage.

"I wonder what they're talking about?" Nick whispered, watching the two men together.

"Oh, you know Vincent," Bubs whispered back, "he's probably remembering a cousin of his from Jersey who always wanted to be a truck driver or something."

Nick thought about what the Rafferty twins had said. Funny, kind, gentle Vincent, a monster? How could they be so blind? By the time Vincent returned to the funeral home, Sam and Willie had run into their house to hide.

"I don't feel like fooling around in here anymore," Nick said.

"It's time for Moose's favorite cartoon shows, anyway," Bubs replied. "He gets depressed when he misses them. I'll help you bring this stuff in before I go." The two friends gathered up the remains of their lunch and the old bookbag, then headed back toward the house. As they walked up the back steps, they heard Vincent's friendly voice.

"Hold on there, Heckle and Jeckle. Come on down here a second," he called. Nick froze on the stairs. He bit down on the inside of his lip. He didn't want to talk to anyone right now, especially Vincent.

"Come on, Nick," Bubs coaxed, "let's go see

what he wants. Maybe he found something out, talking to the enemy."

"He doesn't even know *they are* the enemy," Nick said. He turned around and headed back down the stairs. Vincent was in the long room below the chapel, where the caskets were kept on display. He had just placed the Embassy in the middle of the room and was busy unwrapping the plastic cover. Seeing caskets had never bothered Nick, since he had grown up around them. But now he found he hated the sight of them.

"We've got some real nice neighbors," Vincent said. He lifted the lid of the Embassy. The inside had a cream-colored velvet lining. "Did you meet the twins, Nick? And did you see their father's truck?" Nick dug his fingernails into his old bookbag and lowered his eyes to the floor.

"What's up with him?" Vincent asked Bubs. "Here, why don't each of you go buy yourself a glass of lemonade. It's good stuff." Vincent reached into his pocket and pulled out two quarters.

"We can't," Bubs said.

"Why not?" Vincent asked.

Bubs hesitated, looking from Nick to Vincent. "We, er . . . we can't drink enemy lemonade," he finally muttered.

"Enemy lemonade? What are you talking about? Who's the enemy?" Vincent asked. Nick's lip began to quiver and he tried not to cry.

"The Raffertys, that's who," he croaked.

"Will somebody please tell me what's going on?" Vincent demanded. "Since when did the Raffertys become your enemies?"

"Since they called us weird and creepy for having a funeral home," Nick blurted.

"Oh, so that's it," Vincent said, putting his arm around Nick's shoulder. He led him over to some chairs on the side of the room.

"I don't see what's so weird about having a funeral home," Bubs said, following them.

"That's because you're used to it," Nick replied, fighting back the tears. "They think we're all weird, Vince, like the Addams family or something. They think all this is creepy," he cried, waving his hand at the room full of caskets. "Why can't Uncle Walter have a job like everyone else? Why can't he be a doctor or a truck driver, something normal?"

"Now hold on right there," Vincent said, his voice calm and steady. "Since when was dying not normal? Last time I checked, just about everybody I knew was either planning on doing it or had already done it. Dying happens to be the normal thing to do. It's as normal as getting born. Now, take doctors," Vincent continued. "They deliver babies all the time, helping new life come into the world, and they aren't considered weird, are they? So why shouldn't it be considered normal to help with the ones who are leaving? Just as many people have to leave this world as come into it, you know."

"But why don't other people see it that way?" Nick asked.

"We all see things differently," Vincent explained. "And I guess some people aren't too comfortable with death. They don't see it as part of a natural cycle, this coming and going, and so they're afraid of it."

"But, Vince, they said mean things about us. About you, too," Nick protested. "That has to make them our enemies, doesn't it?"

"Let me tell you about enemies, kiddo," Vincent sighed. "They're a lot of work. Hating someone takes a lot of energy."

"Huh?" Nick didn't understand.

"Hate is a powerful feeling," Vincent explained. "As powerful as love, only the feeling is bad, not good. Do you want to give these people that much feeling? Look, they probably said those things because they don't understand. They made a mistake. We can't get all riled up about everyone who makes a mistake. You know your aunt and uncle better than anyone, Nick. Is Aunt Marge weird? Is your Uncle Walter creepy?"

Nick shook his head.

"Crabby, not creepy," he said. This brought a smile to Vincent's face.

"Your uncle is a perfectionist. That means he wants everything perfect," Vincent said.

"And that means he gets crabby," Nick added.

"I guess I'd have to agree with you there. But he means well, Nick. He really does care about the families, and he does want to do the best he can. You know, there's nothing worse than things going wrong at a funeral. That's why your uncle is so fussy."

"But how do you stand it when he gets so crabby?" Nick asked. "Doesn't it get to you sometimes? Don't you want to go away, as far away as you can?"

Vincent scratched his chin. "To tell you the

truth," he said, "in the beginning I didn't like your uncle very much, and I thought about going away, but as time went on, and I got to know him, I realized that the crabby stuff came and went, and beneath it, your uncle has a good heart. He just wants everything to run smoothly. The problem is life doesn't always run that way. There are all kinds of kinks and curves to work out. Some people, like your Uncle Walter, have a harder time handling the kinks than others."

"Go on, get out of here!" a voice shouted from the yard. Nick recognized Uncle Walter's supercrabby voice. Next came a woman's piercing scream. Nick, Vincent, and Bubs sprang from their chairs and ran up the stairs to the doorway. They looked out and saw Uncle Walter chasing a cocker spaniel around the fountain with a hose. Meanwhile, out on the sidewalk, a young woman who had been jogging stood sopping wet. Unfortunately, she had run right into the water coming from Uncle Walter's hose.

"Would you call that a kink, Vince?" Nick whispered as they listened to the jogger shriek at Uncle Walter.

"Um, that's a kink, all right," Vincent said.

Later that night, Nick lay in bed staring at his trucker calendar. He couldn't stop thinking about his talk with Vincent. He wondered if he'd ever stop hating the Raffertys. He knew that Vincent was right about a lot of things, and he had to admit his feelings were pretty powerful when he thought about the hurtful things the twins had said. But how was he supposed to stop those powerful feelings? And what about Uncle Walter? He giggled now, remembering the horrible look on his uncle's face when the soggy jogger threatened to sue the funeral home.

Then he thought of all the other times Uncle Walter had made him feel so bad. If his uncle did have a good heart, as Vincent said, why didn't Nick know it? In the bright moonlight, the silver-streaked red cab in the picture stood waiting for him, beckoning him to come for a ride. Nick smiled as he closed his eyes and slid behind the wheel.

Chapter Ten

"We've got a cookie for you, Nick," a little voice squeaked by Nick's bed on Friday morning. Nick cracked open one eye. A doll dressed in a dark red evening gown stood smiling at him. Her arms were outstretched, and she was holding a burnt lump of dough. Emily had gotten a Little Miss Muffet oven for her birthday the month before, and she had yet to make a batch of cookies that didn't burn.

Nick took a whiff of the burnt cookie and closed his eyes. "Get that thing away from my bed," he moaned.

"Don't be icky, Nicky," the little voice continued as the doll wobbled from side to side. The cookie fell onto the pillow, disintegrating into a pile of crumbs. Emily's little hand maneuvered the doll, trying to make her scoop up the crumbs.

"Go away, Emily," Nick groaned, sliding under his pillow. Emily giggled from the floor, where she was kneeling beside the bed.

"But Firefly wants you to have your cookie," Emily whispered, pushing the doll under the pillow, close to Nick's ear.

"That's the stupidest name I ever heard," Nick muttered.

"Now don't be icky, Nicky. Firefly wants to give you something," Emily cooed, poking the doll against his ear.

"If old Firefly doesn't get away from my ear, she's going to be missing a head," Nick warned. But Firefly continued to nuzzle his ear. Unable to stand it any longer, Nick swung his arm out and grabbed the doll from Emily's hand. He flung her across the room.

"Firefly!" Emily screamed, as her doll landed with a splash in the aquarium on Nick's bookcase. Nick pushed back the rest of his covers and sat up. "Wow, how did I do that?" he wondered.

"Get her out! Get her out!" Emily shrieked, running over to the aquarium. Emily was afraid of the fish and wouldn't put her hand in the water.

"OK, OK, calm down." Nick jumped out of bed.

"I'm telling Mom what you did," Emily wailed. She watched a guppy swim under the doll's nose. Nick began to laugh as the doll slowly sank to the bottom of the aquarium, her crimson evening gown ballooning around her.

"What's the big deal? So she takes a little bath," he said, reaching into the tank and pulling out the dripping doll.

"Look at her dress. It's ruined!" Emily cried. "And it's all your fault."

"What is going on?" a deep voice demanded. Nick winced and spun around. Uncle Walter was marching into the room. Emily held up the dripping Firefly, who had a long, slimy green plant plastered to the side of her head.

"He ruined my doll," she wailed. "He threw her into his aquarium."

"What did we tell you when we gave you that aquarium?" Uncle Walter said. "You were told to keep the top on at all times, and you were also told only fish were to go in it."

"But, I . . . ," Nick stammered.

"No, buts," Uncle Walter said. "You have got to learn how to behave."

"But she came into my room and was bothering . . ."

"You are three years older than Emily," Uncle Walter snapped. "It's up to you to set the example. How many times do I have to tell you that? I will not put up with this behavior. Everyone in this household is expected to act responsibly, with good sense and proper decorum. Do you understand?" Nick looked at the carpet. Then he stole a glance at the *Babe* on the calendar and imagined himself cruising down the highway with the roar of the engine in his ear.

"How are we supposed to trust you, when you do things like this, Nick?" Nick shrugged. He knew it was no use answering, since Uncle Walter liked to answer these kinds of questions himself. "We can't trust you, no we can't," he continued. "When are you going to learn to act mature? When?" Just then, the phone rang.

"Nick, telephone for you," Aunt Marge called. "It's Bernard Trauffman." Nick looked at Uncle Walter. He was glad that his uncle couldn't read his mind. If he could, he'd see the biggest kink yet. A kink by the name of Slim Jim Trauffman!

As soon as Uncle Walter motioned for him to go, Nick ran out of the room and down the stairs. He picked up the hall phone and stretched the cord into the den, where he hoped no one could hear him.

"Hi, Bernard," Nick said into the receiver, "what's up?"

"That's what I want to know," Bernard answered. "How's the funeral coming along? What have you got planned so far?"

Nick frowned. He hadn't planned anything yet. "Uh, we did get a new casket in," he whispered. "It's called the Embassy. I think Slim would look really good in it."

"How about music?" Bernard asked. "You said something about live music in the chapel." Nick fidgeted with the phone wire. Why had he promised music? He couldn't very well hire a real musician, that would cost money. Suddenly he thought of Bubs.

"We're going to have a trumpet solo. It'll be really good," he promised.

"A trumpet?" Bernard sounded dubious.

"Look, Bernard, this is a respectable funeral home," Nick whispered, mimicking Uncle Walter's serious tone. "We have decorum here."

"What's that?" Bernard asked. "Is that like deodorant?" Nick had no idea what decorum was. He only knew that it was one of Uncle Walter's favorite words.

"Yeah, it's sort of like that," he replied, then quickly changed the subject. "And you promise to pay me the money as soon as the funeral's over?"

"Sure, sure," Bernard agreed. "But what about guests?"

"Guests?"

"Yeah, you know, mourners."

"Bernard, I told you, this has to be a secret funeral. Besides there are going to be plenty of mourners there."

"Like who?" Bernard demanded.

"Well, like you and me and Bubs."

"You and Bubs didn't know Slim the way I did and the way Ian did," Bernard told him.

"Ian?"

"Ian Mettly. He knew Slim Jim since he was a baby snake, no bigger than a worm. I think Slim would want Ian there."

Nick rolled his eyes. Ian Mettly was as nerdy and stuck-up as Bernard. He was also a scratcher. There was always a spot on his arms or legs that he'd scratch until little streams of blood began to run.

"I should be able to have one guest," Bernard demanded.

"OK," Nick agreed, "but only if he promises not to scratch himself while he's in the chapel. My uncle is really fussy about his chairs and his rug."

"He won't scratch, I promise," said Bernard. "I'll tell him to wear long pants and a sweatshirt. So when does it start?"

"The funeral will be tomorrow morning at ten o'clock," Nick told him. "So you'd better have Slim Jim here by nine-thirty. Bring him to my hideout. It's under the big tree on the side yard by the hedge. You can invite Ian, but no one else. This has to be a secret funeral, you understand?"

Chapter Eleven

"**Y**ou have to invite me," Emily demanded, as she walked into the den.

"To what?" Nick asked, hanging up the phone.

"You know," Emily grinned, "to the funeral."

"Shh . . ." Nick's eyes grew wide. "Were you spying on me? You were, weren't you?"

"So what if I was?" Emily sniffed. "You threw Firefly into the aquarium."

"But that was an accident," Nick protested.

"It doesn't matter," Emily objected, smoothing out the wrinkles on Firefly's wet dress. "Now you have to let me come, to make up for it."

"Em the Phlem," Nick muttered. "Emily,

you don't understand. This is a secret funeral. No one is supposed to know. Not Grammy, not your mom, not your dad. You just can't come."

"Oh, yes, I can," said Emily. "And if you don't let me, I'll tell everyone about it, and then it won't be a secret anymore."

Nick gritted his teeth. "Emily, this is a special secret funeral. Everyone coming is going to be older than you."

"We don't care," Emily insisted. "We still want to come."

"We? Who else have you told?" Nick's voice was panicky.

"Firefly heard you talking about it, too. So she wants to come, but I'll have to get her a better dress." Nick rolled his eyes.

"All right, Emily," he sighed, "you can come." Emily held Firefly up to his face. "You can both come. But you have to promise not to tell anyone else, not Grammy or Vincent or anyone. Do you understand?"

"Yes, but who's the funeral for?" Emily asked.

"It's a funeral for Bernard Trauffman's snake, Slim Jim," Nick told her. Emily wrinkled her nose. Nick held his breath, hoping that she'd change her mind.

"As long as we don't have to touch him, we'll come," Emily decided.

Nick spent the rest of the morning setting up the chairs that had been returned from the Bingo Bash. For once, he didn't mind the work, as it gave him a perfect excuse to be in the chapel.

When Nick was sure that Uncle Walter and Vincent were nowhere in sight, he removed the Oriental rug that covered the trapdoor. He lifted the door and peered down. He could see the Embassy sitting on a cart in the center of the casket room. Nick knew that he would need Bubs to help him push the Embassy onto the hydraulic lift. Nick would also have to light the candles. He closed the trapdoor and re-placed the rug. Then he went to the back closet and found the box of matches that Uncle Walter kept there. They were extra long, especially made for lighting candles. Uncle Walter had given him a lesson on using them, and Nick knew that he would have to be careful and not let anyone else touch them.

He closed the closet door and scanned the room again. Everything seemed perfect and ready for tomorrow's service. Nick looked through the doorway and caught a glimpse of

Vincent watering the bright yellow flowers that circled the fountain.

Oh, no, I forgot about Vincent! he thought. What if he's coming to work on Saturday? Even though Vincent was understanding, he was still a grown-up, and a grown-up who worked for Uncle Walter. If Vincent was going to work on Saturday, there wasn't much chance that Slim Jim would be resting in peace at the Wiloby Funeral Home. Nick walked outside and sauntered over to the fountain. He shot a glance at Uncle Walter, who was busy spraying bug killer on the dogwood tree.

Vincent playfully squirted the hose in Nick's direction. Nick jumped out of the way. "I'm taking your aunt and uncle to the airport tonight. Do you want to come along for the ride?" Vincent asked.

"Sure, I guess so," Nick replied. "When's Grammy coming?"

"Your aunt Marge left a little while ago to pick her up at the bus station."

"What about you?" Nick asked. "What are you doing this weekend?"

"Well, I was going to see about laying that sidewalk around the side entrance . . ." Nick's smile began to droop. "But then my cousin,

Frankie G., called last night . . ." Vincent paused. Nick held his breath. "You remember, the one I was telling you about, the one who lives in Atlantic City? Well, he's planning on coming to visit for the weekend. So I thought we might try some fishing down by the creek."

"Fishing!" Nick exclaimed. "With your cousin, Frankie G. Gee, Vince, that sounds like fun."

"Are you fishing for an invitation?" Vincent smiled.

"Oh, no," Nick replied, shaking his head. "I'd like to, but I've got some stuff I've got to do."

"What kind of stuff?" Vincent asked.

"Oh, some friends are dropping by." Nick shrugged, trying to look as innocent as he could. "I'm glad *you* can go, though," he said, his voice brimming over with enthusiasm. Vincent gave him a funny look. But before he could ask any questions, Nick spun around and headed for the house. He ran at top speed up the stairs and into the kitchen, where he dialed Bubs's number. He made a mental checklist in his head. The chairs were set up and ready to go, the new fancy Embassy casket was empty, Vincent was going fishing, and Aunt Marge was picking up Grammy. She and Uncle Walter would be leaving later that night. The only thing left was the music.

"Hello?" Bubs's voice came on the line.

"Hi, Bubs, how's your trumpet?" Nick asked.

"My what?" Bubs asked.

"Your trumpet," Nick repeated. "Listen, Bubs, I need a favor. I need you to play your trumpet at Slim's funeral."

"What are you talking about?" Bubs cried. "I haven't even had one lesson yet."

"That's OK," Nick assured him. "The music is just for background stuff. No one will be listening."

"But I don't even know how to play," Bubs complained.

"What's to know?" Nick shrugged. "All you do is hold it up and blow it."

"That's easy for you to say," Bubs grumbled.

" 'On the Road with Nick and Bubs,' " Nick whispered into the phone. "That could be us. Once I get that *Truckers' Road Atlas*, we can map out our route. Then when we're old enough, we can cruise all the way to Florida to pick up those peanuts. And if we have a sleeper cab, we can take Moose along."

"He wouldn't come unless there was a TV," Bubs remarked.

"So, we'll get one of those little TVs." Nick's voice rose with excitement. "Can't you just picture it? We'll be cruising down the highway, with me at the wheel. You'll be sitting beside me, reading the maps, and stuffing peanuts into your mouth, and good old Moose will be in the back, watching Road Runner cartoons on his very own little TV, with his two-tone tail hanging out the window. Can't you just picture it?"

"Yeah, yeah. And when I grow up, I'm going to be a brain surgeon, but I still don't want to play the trumpet tomorrow."

"I'll give you my fossil rock," Nick pleaded. No response. "And my wax lips."

"What time should I bring the trumpet?" Bubs whispered into the phone.

Chapter Twelve

"Where are Aunt Marge and Grammy?" Nick asked Uncle Walter a few hours later. His uncle was in the kitchen making lunch.

"They're having a ladies' day out," Uncle Walter told him. He spread some tuna fish onto a piece of bread. "Your aunt wanted to pick up a few last-minute things for our trip, so she and Grammy were planning on going shopping after the bus station."

Nick grinned. He loved it when his grandmother came to visit. Unlike Uncle Walter, Grammy Robbins was always smiling and laughing, and she had a way of making the most boring chore seem like fun.

"I can just hear Grammy saying, 'I read my horoscope and it said that today was a good day to shop.'"

"Your grandmother doesn't go anywhere without reading her horoscope," said Uncle Walter.

"But she always expects good things to happen. Even if her horoscope says something bad is going to happen, Grammy can twist it around so it sounds good."

"That's because she's an optimist," said Uncle Walter.

"Like Emily," Nick replied.

"Um, I guess you're right. Emily is a lot like your grandmother." While Nick stood wondering who he was like, his uncle asked him to go and call Emily for lunch.

Nick found his cousin in the living room, drawing a picture with her colored markers. He squinted and looked at the picture. There was a big, smiling, blobby thing in the center of the page surrounded by blue waves.

"What are you making that for?" Nick asked.

"It's for Grammy," Emily told him. "I want to make her a picture before she gets here. Do you think it's good enough?"

Nick cocked his head and took another look. Then he turned the picture upside down. "That looks better," he said.

"No, not that way!" Emily yelled. "You've

got Grammy upside down!" She reached over and turned the picture around.

"Oh, I thought it was supposed to be a picture from outer space." Nick grinned. "You mean that's not the earth?"

"No, that's Grammy," Emily told him. "She's swimming at the pool. Can't you see all the flowers on her bathing suit?"

"Flowers? They look like mountains to me," Nick said, heading back to the kitchen. "Come on, it's time to . . ." But before he could finish he heard the doorbell ring. He looked out the big picture window and saw a skinny girl of about fourteen standing on the balcony. She had reddish-brown hair, except for her bangs, which were a dark blue. Nick decided she must be Carrie Rafferty. But what was she doing at their house? Nick thought about not answering the door, until he heard Uncle Walter calling from the kitchen.

The door swung open and Carrie Rafferty rushed into the room.

"I'm sorry," she apologized. Then she burst into tears. "Our phone hasn't been connected yet, and my dad is on the road," she cried. "It's my mom. She's in a lot of pain. The baby is coming, and we've got to get her to the hospital."

Nick looked over at Emily who was standing behind the couch. She looked as nervous as he did.

"I'll get my uncle," he said, racing out of the room.

"Uncle Walter," he cried, "come quick, Mrs. Rafferty is having her baby, and Mr. Rafferty isn't home." Uncle Walter dropped the knife into the tuna-fish bowl and hurried into the living room. Carrie was pacing back and forth, still crying.

"Don't worry, everything will be all right," Uncle Walter told her. "I'll call for an ambulance, and then I'll be right over. Stay with your mother until I get there," he ordered.

Carrie ran out of the house as Uncle Walter ran for the phone. Before his uncle could finish dialing, Sam and Willie appeared at the door.

"My mom said to hurry!" Sam cried.

"She doesn't think there's time to wait for the ambulance," Willie added, trying to catch his breath. Uncle Walter hung up the phone.

"Tell her we're coming," he said. He opened the door leading to the funeral home and shouted for Vincent.

"OK, I'm coming," Vincent called. "What's all the hullabaloo? Is lunch ready?"

"No, the Raffertys' baby is ready," Uncle Walter told him.

"Huh?"

"We don't have much time," Uncle Walter said. He grabbed Vincent's arm. "Am I ever glad you're here. Do you remember that cousin of yours in New Jersey, the one who had the baby you helped deliver last year?"

"Sure, my cousin Angela," Vincent said. "That was a close call. We were in their car, on our way for some pizza, Angela loves pizza, when all of a sudden . . ."

"Not now, Vincent," Uncle Walter interrupted. "I just need to know if you remember any of the details of the delivery."

"Yeah, I guess so, but . . ."

"That will have to be good enough," Uncle Walter said. "Marge has the car, so we'll have to use the hearse. Mrs. Rafferty can lie down, so that will be better anyway. We might be able to get to the hospital in time, but in case we don't, what do you think you'll need for the baby?" Vincent nodded, as if he finally understood what was going on.

"I don't know, I guess we could use some

towels and a blanket and . . ." he yelled, running toward the bathroom.

"Meet me out front as soon as you can," Uncle Walter called over his shoulder. He raced out of the house. Nick stared at the open door, wondering what he should do. He still felt as if the Raffertys were the enemy, but he also felt worried about the baby.

Nick could hear the garage doors open and the sound of the hearse's engine. He and Emily went to the window. The hearse was pulling out of the driveway.

"Do you think Mrs. Rafferty's baby is going to be all right?" Emily whispered. They watched Vincent dash through the door and down the steps, carrying a bundle of towels.

"I don't know," Nick whispered back, "let's go see." He reached for Emily's hand. Together the two followed Vincent over to the Raffertys' house. While Vincent and Uncle Walter went inside, Nick and Emily waited on the grass. They could see Sam and Willie and Annie huddled together on the Raffertys' front porch. Annie sat whimpering between Sam and Willie, who looked as if they might start crying at any moment. Suddenly the front door opened, and Mrs. Rafferty came out, supported by Uncle Walter on one side and Vincent on the other. Carrie was behind them, carrying a suitcase.

"Oh, good, Nick, I'm glad you're here," Uncle Walter called. "Vincent and I are taking Mrs. Rafferty to the hospital. We can't wait for the ambulance. Carrie is coming with us to be with her mother. So I'm leaving you in charge. Take all the kids over to our house and wait there. Your aunt Marge should be getting home soon. I can depend on you to look after things, can't I, Nick?"

Nick gulped and nodded. For once his uncle was asking him a question that he wanted Nick to answer himself.

"We'll call you from the hospital." Mrs. Rafferty struggled to smile at the twins and Annie. "Be good while I'm gone. Everything's going to be all right," she tried to assure them, although her smile turned into a grimace as she leaned on Uncle Walter, clutching his sleeve.

"Oh, I don't know if I can make it," she whimpered. The twins' eyes filled with tears.

"Don't worry, we'll get you there in time," Uncle Walter said. "It's going to be all right, I promise." Mrs. Rafferty seemed to relax a bit, and Uncle Walter and Vincent were able to get her into the hearse. Vincent and Carrie climbed in with her, and Uncle Walter got behind the wheel. Nick and the others stood in silence as they watched the hearse speed away. No one spoke, until Annie began to cry.

"I want Mommy, I want Mommy," she wailed.

"Your mom is going to be OK," Nick consoled her.

"What if they don't get to the hospital in time?" Willie whispered. A big tear rolled down his cheek.

"She's got Uncle Walter and Vincent with her. They'll take good care of her, you'll see," Nick told him. "Vincent delivered a baby in a car just last year."

"He did?" Sam looked surprised. "Whose baby was it?"

"It was his cousin's baby," Nick said. "She lives in New Jersey. Vincent's got hundreds of cousins who live in New Jersey. When we get to my house, I'll tell you all about them. Hey, do you guys like tuna fish?" Sam and Willie nodded. Annie made a face between sniffles.

"I don't like tuna fish, either," Emily said, offering to take Annie's hand. "We can have peanut butter and jelly, if you'd like." Annie wiped her eyes and smiled.

"So that makes three tuna-fish sandwiches and two peanut butter and jellys," Nick said. They walked across the yard and up the steps to the kitchen. Emily and Annie took their sandwiches to Emily's room, so they could have lunch with her dolls. Nick and the twins sat at the kitchen table and ate tuna-fish sandwiches, pickles, Cheezios, olives, and strawberry ice cream. As they waited for the phone to ring, they discussed names for the baby.

"He needs a good name," Sam said, dipping his pickle into the box of strawberry ice cream. "Something that sounds strong, like Conar."

"Or Mongo," Willie suggested.

"Mongo Rafferty? Um, that's pretty good, but it sounds a little like a dog," Nick said. He dipped his Cheezio into the ice cream and topped it with an olive. "What do your parents want to name him?"

"Oh, something dumb like Daniel or Robert," said Sam.

"Mom said that it's her turn to pick out the name, since Dad named Annie. They take turns. Mom said she'll wait until he's born and then decide." It sounded like everyone was expecting the new baby to be a boy. The twins especially wanted a brother.

After lunch, everyone moved into the living room. The boys set up a marble run on the rug, and Emily and Annie came down to play with dolls on the coffee table.

Aunt Marge couldn't have been more surprised when she and Grammy Robbins walked into the house and found a room full of Rafferty children. Nick was about to explain, but the phone rang.

"Good afternoon, the Wiloby Funeral Home," Aunt Marge said into the receiver. Nick, the twins, Emily, and Annie all sat holding their breaths. Aunt Marge's mouth dropped open.

"Why, yes, I certainly will tell them," she exclaimed, looking more and more surprised. She hung up the phone and turned to the twins and Annie. "That was your sister Carrie. She said to tell you that your mother and your new baby brother are fine!"

"Yahoo!" Sam cheered.

"It seems they didn't make it to the hospital in time, but everyone is OK."

"What's the baby's name?" Willie asked. "Did they give him his name?"

"Why, yes," Aunt Marge said, with a somewhat bewildered look on her face, "his name is Vincent!"

Chapter Thirteen

Later that night, everyone piled into the car for the drive to the airport. They were still talking about the arrival of Vincent Walter Rafferty. Mrs. Rafferty had decided to give her baby the middle name of Walter, since Uncle Walter provided such excellent transportation to the hospital—even if it was a bit unusual.

Nick was sitting in the backseat with Aunt Marge and Grammy Robbins. Emily was in the front seat between Uncle Walter and Vincent. Aunt Marge was going over all the things that Grammy "should know" while they were gone. How to answer the phone, how to get in touch with them in case of an emergency, and how to activate the sprinkler system in case of a fire.

"It can be turned on manually," Aunt Marge told her. "Walter and Vincent are waiting for some parts to fix the automatic mechanism."

"I'm sure everything will be fine," Grammy assured her, "although, according to my horoscope for next week, a dramatic event is about to occur that could have an important effect on my career."

"But, Frances, you've been retired for ten years," Uncle Walter reminded her.

"Um, that's true," Grammy agreed. "But I did make pot holders for the senior center's craft fair that's taking place tomorrow. My friend Edna is going to be selling them for me at her table. It might have something to do with that. I didn't sell too many last year."

"Maybe someone will go to the fair and buy all the pot holders you made," Nick suggested.

"Now that *would* be dramatic." Grammy laughed. "And if that happens, I'll have to come back and take you and Emily out for ice-cream sundaes. You'd better start thinking about what flavors you'd like."

"Chocolate," Emily cried.

"Strawberry," Nick said.

"I just hope nothing more dramatic than that

happens while we're gone." Aunt Marge frowned.

"Marge, you worry too much," Uncle Walter said. Nick couldn't believe his ears. It was usually his uncle who was the worrier. He had never seen Uncle Walter so relaxed.

"Darn, I think I missed the turn," Vincent said. He slowed down.

"Don't worry, Vincent," Uncle Walter said, "it's not like anyone here is having a baby. You can turn around at the next exit."

Ordinarily, a missed turn would be a kink for Uncle Walter. But instead of his usual crabby grumbling, Uncle Walter was actually enjoying himself. Nick looked from Vincent to his uncle and realized how proud he was of both of them. They're heroes, he thought. Nick had never in his wildest dreams imagined Uncle Walter as a hero. But since he had come home from the hospital, Uncle Walter had changed. He'd been making jokes and looking relaxed. Could he really have changed for good? Nick knew that the characters in his comic books were always undergoing incredible transformations. Maybe this was like that, he thought. Maybe Uncle Walter the Grumbler had been transformed into Uncle Walter the Heroic!

At the airport, however, Uncle Walter's sunny mood disappeared after he discovered that the seats he had booked for the flight were assigned to someone else.

"What do you mean you don't have any aisle seats left? I specifically requested an aisle seat. This is no way to run a business," Uncle Walter fumed.

So much for incredible transformations, Nick thought. When it finally came time to say good-bye, however, Nick was surprised to hear Uncle Walter say, "Help Grammy keep an eye on Emily, Nick. I know I can depend on you after the way you handled things today."

"Today? Me?" Nick asked.

"Yes, you." Uncle Walter laid his hand on Nick's shoulder. "You took charge of things when you looked after all the kids. It's good to know that I can leave and not worry about you getting into trouble." Nick tried to smile, but the image of Slim Jim lying in Uncle Walter's top-of-the-line Embassy casket stopped him. Aunt Marge leaned over and gave him a hug and kiss.

"Have fun while we're gone," she said. She hugged Emily and Grammy, too.

"And keep an eye on the place," Uncle Walter called with a wink. Nick wasn't sure whether he was winking at him or at Vincent.

"We will, we will." Vincent answered for both of them.

Nick sat quietly in the front seat with Vincent on the ride home, while Emily chattered to Grammy about her dolls and Firefly's dive into the aquarium. All Nick could think of was Uncle Walter.

"What's on your mind, kiddo?" Vincent asked finally.

"I was just wondering about some things," Nick said.

"What kind of things?"

"Well, people, I guess. Do you think people ever change in a big way, Vince? Could they change so much that you'd hardly know them anymore?"

"Hmmm, I don't know about that," Vincent replied, "but I think sometimes we change the way we look at people, and that makes them look different. Take our new neighbors, for example."

"They saw you as a monster a few days ago," Nick said.

"Right," Vincent nodded. "And now, look, they're naming their baby after me!"

"Oh, I get it," Nick said, shaking his head. "You didn't change, they just changed the way they saw you." Suddenly Nick remembered what Vincent had said about Uncle Walter having a good heart.

"Maybe Uncle Walter is changing the way he looks at me, and I think I might be changing the way I look at him," mused Nick.

"Sounds like a lot of changing going on." Vincent chuckled. "I, myself, plan on making some changes this weekend."

"What kind of changes?" Nick asked.

"Every time my cousin Frankie G. and I go fishing together, he catches the biggest fish. Well, the boy is due for a change. This weekend I plan on catching the biggest, fattest trout you ever saw. And to make sure that I do, I stopped at the sporting goods shop and picked up some new lures. They're guaranteed to bring in the big ones."

"What's the biggest fish you ever caught, Vince?" Nick asked.

"Oh, well, let me see," Vincent said, cocking his head. "I guess that would be the fish I caught while I was out on my cousin Tony's boat down by Hoboken. That fish was so big that when we pulled it in, it sunk our boat, sunk it straight down to the bottom of the river. And you know what's at the bottom of the Hudson River, don't you?" He and Vincent spent the rest of the ride home spinning a tale about the biggest fish ever caught off the shores of Hoboken, New Jersey.

I hope Vincent never changes, Nick thought as they drove into the Wiloby Funeral Home parking lot.

Chapter Fourteen

On Saturday morning the world seemed in perfect harmony to Nick Robbins. As he looked out the bathroom window, the grass seemed greener, the birds sang more sweetly, and even the two dogs drinking at Uncle Walter's fountain seemed special.

It's the perfect day for old Slim Jim's funeral, he thought. Aunt Marge and Uncle Walter are off on a trip, Vincent is busy catching the biggest trout he can, and Grammy is sewing in the den. With so many things going right, what could possibly go wrong?

Just then the doorbell rang. Nick brushed his teeth and raced down the stairs to find the Rafferty twins waiting in the living room.

"Looks like we're going to be having some

company today, Nick," Grammy Robbins called from the den. "Mr. Rafferty asked if the kids could spend the day here."

"All day?" Nick gasped, looking through the doorway. Annie and Emily were standing beside Grammy at the sewing machine.

"The whole day," Sam said.

"Dad and Carrie are visiting Mom and the baby, and then they're going shopping for a new washing machine and some baby stuff," Willie piped up. "Why don't we go outside and make a volcano?" Nick's shoulders slumped. Any other day, he would have been glad to make a volcano with the twins. He shifted nervously from foot to foot, wondering how he was going to keep his promise to Bernard and go through with the funeral, without letting the Raffertys in on the secret. He would have to swear them to secrecy.

"Let's go out to my hideout," he whispered, turning toward the door. They followed him out and crawled behind him underneath the branches. As soon as they were quiet, Nick told them about the plans for the funeral.

"You can't ever tell anyone, not your mother or father or anyone," he ordered. "This is a secret funeral, do you understand?"

Sam and Willie nodded. "You're really going to bury a snake in one of your uncle's coffins?" whispered Sam.

"Uncle Walter calls them caskets, and we're not going to bury him," Nick explained. "He'll just be in it for the service, and then we'll take him out. Uncle Walter will never know the difference."

"But what if he does?" asked Willie. "What if your uncle finds out?"

"Then there will be another funeral for you to go to, mine," Nick said.

The twins followed closely behind Nick as he snuck back into the house. He could hear the purr of the sewing machine coming from the den. Carefully, he opened the door leading to the funeral home. The three boys made their way down the stairs as quietly as they could.

"Are we there yet?" Willie croaked in the darkness. "Are we in the coffin room yet?"

"Almost," whispered Nick. "Follow me." They walked through a hallway and down another set of stairs to the long room. Nick turned on the lights, and the twins saw the roomful of caskets.

"Oooo . . . it's like being in a creepy movie," Willie cried.

"A vampire movie," Sam whispered, clutching his brother's arm.

"Which one?" Willie squeaked. "Which one is the snake going in?"

Nick walked up to the Embassy and knelt down beside it. "Slim's going in style," he whispered. "This is the best we've got."

"What are you doing?" Sam asked.

"I'm releasing the brakes on the cart," Nick explained. "This way we can wheel it over to the lift. The chapel is right above us." He unlocked both brakes, then began to push the cart across the room. Sam and Willie stood side by side, not daring to move.

"Are you two going to help me or not?" Nick asked, giving the cart another push.

"I . . . I . . . don't want to touch it." Willie's voice was quivery with fear.

"Me . . . me . . . neither," Sam said.

Nick rolled his eyes and groaned. "Oh, come on you two . . ." Just then a loud bark came from the front yard.

"That sounds like Moose," he whispered, running up the stairs. He opened the chapel door and saw Bubs tying Moose to the hemlock tree. The old trumpet was tucked under his arm.

"Bubs, in here," Nick called, keeping his voice as low as he could, but Bubs had ducked into the hideout.

"Come on," Nick whispered to the others. "We've got to go get Bubs." The boys raced across the yard and hurried into the hideout.

"What are they doing here?" Bubs asked, nodding at the twins. "I thought they were the enemy."

Nick told Bubs about the events leading up to the birth of Vincent Walter Rafferty, and how he and the twins had become friends again. He got so carried away telling the story, he lost track of the time. Before he knew it, Bernard Trauffman was standing outside the hideout.

"Nick, hey, Nick," Bernard called.

"Oh, no!" cried Nick. "Bernard's here, and I haven't got anything ready." He stuck his head between the branches.

"Hi, Bernard," Nick grinned. "Great day for a funeral. I'll be right out." He turned to his friends. "We've got a lot to do, and we've got to do it fast," he whispered. "Bubs, you and I will get Slim ready," he ordered. "Sam, you and Willie pick some flowers from the yard. Meet us back at the chapel as soon as you can."

Bernard looked surprised when he saw the Rafferty twins coming out of the hideout, but Nick explained quickly that they'd be working as his "assistants."

"I'll wait here for Ian," Bernard said, handing Nick the coffee can. There was still some dirt on the plastic lid. Bernard had dug it up from the ground only minutes earlier. Nick brushed off the dirt and gave Bernard a solemn look.

"You wait in the hideout. I'll send my assistants for you when we're ready to begin the service," he said. His voice sounded smooth and velvety, the way Uncle Walter's got when he was conducting a funeral. Bernard nodded and ducked under the branches to wait. Meanwhile Nick and his assistants raced across the yard.

While Sam and Willie picked flowers, Nick and Bubs discussed the best way to arrange Slim Jim's remains in the casket. They decided to place a paper towel on the bottom to protect the Embassy's cream-colored interior. While Nick looked for paper towels in the closet, Emily appeared on the stairs.

"Did Grammy see you come down here?" he demanded.

"No," Emily retorted, "she and Annie are working on Annie's doll dress."

"Well, you've got to go back up," Nick told her. "We're not ready. Come back in ten minutes."

"OK, but we *are* coming back," she said firmly, turning to leave.

"Only if you're sure Grammy won't miss you, and Annie swears to keep it a secret," Nick called. He leaned on the cart that held the casket and told Bubs to push.

"This is heavy," Bubs groaned, as the cart moved forward.

"We've only got to get it over to the lift," Nick told him.

"It's a good thing there is a lift, or we'd never get it up the stairs," Bubs mumbled. They pushed the cart onto the lift's platform. Nick set the brakes so the casket wouldn't roll away, and then reached for the coffee can on the floor.

"Go ahead," he whispered, holding it up to Bubs, "you can take Slim out of the can."

"Me?" Bubs asked. "Why should I take him out? You're the one who's in charge."

"But you're my assistant," Nick said.

Bubs shook his head. "I'm not touching a dead snake."

"I wouldn't touch him either," Emily remarked from the stairs.

Nick shot her a dirty look. "I told you to go back upstairs."

"What's that awful smell?" Bubs asked, wrinkling his nose. Nick looked at the can, wondering if it could be Slim Jim. Then he took a whiff of air.

"Emily, are you baking again?" The scent of charred chocolate chip cookies came drifting down the stairs.

"Oh, my gosh, I forgot my cookies!" Emily cried, racing up the steps. "I'll bring you down a plateful."

"Oh, great," Nick moaned, "she's burning a new batch of cookies just for us."

Bubs shrugged.

Nick looked down at the can. "I guess I have to open it." He winced as he lifted the plastic lid.

Chapter Fifteen

"How does he look?" Bubs whispered, inching closer to Nick.

"He looks the same as he always did," Nick said, peering into the coffee can.

"Does he smell?" asked Bubs. Nick took a whiff and wrinkled his nose.

"About as much as usual. He's got that snake smell." Nick reached in quickly, pulled the snake out, and placed him on the paper towel in the casket. Just as Nick was about to stretch him out, he heard the chapel door open.

Nick and Bubs ran up the stairs and saw Sam and Willie standing with a bouquet of bright yellow flowers.

"Where did you pick those?" Nick gasped.

"They were growing around your fountain," Sam said, walking toward Nick.

"We picked all that were there," Willie announced. "Is it enough?"

"Enough!" Nick shrieked. "You picked all of Uncle Walter's special stinky flowers! How could you!"

"But you told us to pick some flowers," Sam protested.

"And you didn't say which ones," Willie added. "They *are* kind of stinky." He frowned, smelling the bright petals. Meanwhile, Bernard and Ian came to the door.

Nick grabbed the flowers from the twins and stuck them into an empty vase that sat on a little table at the front of the room.

"Hi, Nick, we're here," Emily called. She and Annie walked into the chapel. Annie was carrying their dolls, and Emily was balancing a plate of burnt cookies.

"Does Grammy know where you are?" Nick asked, holding his nose.

"No, she said it was a good time of day to watch a little TV. She turned on 'Champion Golf,' and she fell asleep," Emily said, offering a cookie to Sam. Sam took one look at the little burnt mound and wrinkled his nose. Willie did the same.

"Everyone please take a seat on the folding chairs in the front row," said Nick. Ian pulled up his pant leg to scratch at an old scab, but Bernard stopped him before he could get to it.

Nick motioned for Willie to come join him by the curtain on the side of the room. The two whispered for several minutes. Everyone's eyes were on Willie as he walked to the front of the room. As he lifted the Oriental rug and pulled up the trapdoor, a hush fell over the room.

Nick knew that Uncle Walter usually brought the casket up on the lift before the mourners arrived, but having everyone wait for it seemed more dramatic. Nick nodded to Bubs at the back of the room. Bubs lifted the trumpet to his mouth, took a deep breath, and then blew as hard as he could. A harsh sound came out, making everyone jump.

Nick hurriedly pushed back the curtain and pressed the orange button on the wall. There was a loud hum as it activated the hydraulic lift.

"Here he comes," Nick whispered. The humming of the lift grew louder as the long dark casket came into view. A deathly silence fell over the room. Everyone's eyes were on the casket as it rose up higher and higher before them. With a loud creak the lift came to a sudden stop and the casket shifted slightly. The mourners craned their necks to get a look inside. Nick walked over to the casket and signaled for Bubs to stop playing. Everyone clapped with relief. Nick cleared his throat and in a solemn voice said, "Bernard, at this time, if you'd like to, you can come up and say a few words as a final good-bye to Slim Jim." Bernard walked slowly up to the casket and looked inside. He turned around to face everyone, and a tear rolled down his cheek. He took a minute to compose himself before speaking.

"As far as snakes go," Bernard began, "Slim Jim was the best. He was always in a good mood and never nasty. I know I'll never have as good a friend as I had in him." Bernard wiped his eyes, and the girls began to sniffle. Nick had a hard time swallowing. Bernard went on.

"I'm glad I got to give Slim Jim the best funeral a pet ever had, because he *was* the best pet a kid ever had." He sniffled loudly as he looked back into the casket. "I . . . I . . . I just don't think . . ." More sniffling as he took one more look. "I just don't think he's facing the right way."

Nick spun around and peered into the Embassy. Slim Jim was indeed facing the wrong way. His tail rested on the pillow, while his head faced the bottom of the casket.

The rest of the mourners jumped out of their seats and gathered around to have a look at the deceased. As everyone stood gaping, the chapel door slowly opened.

Chapter Sixteen

Two old men, dressed in suits, walked through the door.

"Must be the grandkids," one of the men said, pointing to the group surrounding the casket.

"Hey? What was that?" the other man hollered, cupping his hand to his ear.

"I said, those must be Willard's grandkids," the old man shouted into the other's ear. "Sure am going to miss the old coot." He scanned the group, resting his eyes on Bernard. "See that little chubby one up there? He's the spittin' image of Willard. Yup, he's a Peeps, all right, no doubt about it."

"Don't know about that," the other said. "I left my glasses at home. Can't make out the nose on my face."

"Who are those guys?" Bubs whispered.

"I don't know," Nick gasped, "but I can't let them see Slim Jim or Uncle Walter could find out." Nick took a deep breath and hurried to the back of the room, where the old men were standing.

"Er, excuse me," he began, "but I think you have . . ."

"Have to use your men's room, is what I have to do," one of the old men interrupted. Nick smiled and pointed to the door with an *M* on it. Then he turned back to the remaining stranger.

"I think you have the wrong funeral home," he said.

"Yes, it's a beautiful funeral." The elderly man nodded. "Not that Willard would have wanted any fuss. He wasn't that type, don't you know?"

"No," Nick said, shaking his head, "you don't understand. I think you've come to the wrong funeral home. He's not . . ." The old man stood with his hand cupped to his ear, and when he spoke, his voice was so loud, Nick had to take a step backward.

"Oh, yes, he was certainly liked a lot, Willard Peeps was," the old man shouted. "The boys down at the station house all loved him.

He was fire chief for almost thirty-three years, don't you know? No one ever had a bad word to say about Willard."

"Look, you've got the wrong . . ." Nick shouted.

"Yes, yes, young fella, I guess you're right. I should have a look," the old man muttered, slowly making his way to the front of the room. Nick followed beside him, pulling on his sleeve and trying to coax him back toward the door. With a wrinkled hand, the old man brushed him away.

"Now's not the time for conversation, son," he said. Nick rolled his eyes to the ceiling as the old man stood squinty-eyed, staring into the Embassy. There was a moment of tense silence, while everyone waited for him to scream. But much to their surprise, he didn't say a word. He just shook his shiny bald head and, frowning, started to shuffle back down the aisle. He met his friend coming out of the men's room and reached out for his arm.

"Don't go up, Ralph," he shouted, shaking his head from side to side. "It's not a pretty sight. Old Willard's pretty shriveled up. I didn't realize he had lost so much weight." The two found chairs at the back of the room, and noisily sat down.

"You'd better play something else, and then maybe they'll leave," Nick whispered to Bubs. Bubs brought his trumpet to his lips and began to blow. Everyone covered his or her ears except the two old men sitting in the back. Nick thought that Bubs was playing much worse than before, but then he realized that Bubs was not playing alone. Someone was ringing the bell to the chapel door!

Nick ran to the door and peeked out. A fireman dressed in a long black coat, hat, and shiny black boots was standing on the sidewalk. Three long fire trucks were pulling up in front of the Wiloby Funeral Home.

"Oh, no!" Nick groaned.

Chapter Seventeen

Nick rushed to the casket and slammed down the lid seconds before the other firemen reached the entrance. The children huddled close together as the firemen filed into the chapel.

"What's going on?" Bubs whispered to Nick.

"I don't know," Nick groaned, "but it doesn't look good."

"I thought you said this was supposed to be a secret funeral," Bernard said. Emily and Annie looked as if they were about to cry, and Emily did cry out when she spotted a heavyset fireman sit down on her doll.

"Firefly! Firefly!" she screamed. Just then a loud whooshing sound filled the room. A shower of water rained down from the ceiling.

"Oh, no, someone turned on the sprinklers!" Nick cried. He looked around and saw Grammy Robbins rushing down the stairs, waving a fire extinguisher.

"I guess I got them on all right," she called. "I smelled something burning and then I heard Emily calling fire. Where's the fire?"

The firemen sprang out of their seats and ran up the aisle.

"There's no fire," Nick tried to explain when a burly fireman lifted him into the air.

"Don't be afraid, kid, we'll get you out of here!" the fireman bellowed. He swung Nick over his shoulder.

"But you don't understand," Nick yelled. "It was all a mistake. My cousin was calling Firefly, not . . ." His words were lost as the firemen rushed about, trying to rescue the roomful of mourners.

As Nick was carried out the door, he looked up and saw Willie hanging over the shoulder of another fireman.

"Hey, Nick," Willie yelled, "this is a pretty cool funeral."

"It wasn't supposed to be this cool," Nick said. Everyone, including Grammy Robbins, was carried out of the building.

"Hey, don't forget the chief," one of the firemen yelled back into the chapel.

"Nick, look," Bubs called, "they're even rescuing Slim Jim!" Nick groaned. He watched several firemen exit the chapel, the Embassy hoisted on their strong shoulders. They gently laid the casket on the lawn. A number of cars stopped, and neighbors began to gather to see what was going on.

"Wow, this is pretty cool, Nick," Bernard said. "I never knew a funeral could be this exciting."

"I wish we could have something like this for our dog Sparky," Willie added.

"But Sparky isn't even dead," Sam reminded him.

"Well, maybe we could have one anyway, sort of like a rehearsal," Willie suggested. Nick groaned even louder.

"It's pretty bad, isn't it, Nick?" said Bubs, coming up beside him.

"Bad? Bad would be good!" Nick watched his grandmother talking to a few of the firemen and a woman with a pad and pencil.

"This is way past bad," Nick said. "I don't think it could get much worse."

"Nick," Grammy Robbins called, "come

over here, please." Nick dragged himself to where she was standing beside the casket.

After a thorough search, the firemen concluded that the building was not on fire. With the help of a reporter from the local newspaper, they figured out that they had mistaken the Wiloby Funeral Home for the Whipple Funeral Home in Ackermanville.

"I guess we got confused," one of the firemen admitted, pointing to the fountain. "The fella at Whipple mentioned something about a big fountain he had just put out front, and when we saw your fountain, we . . ." His voice trailed off as he looked down at his boots, too embarrassed to go on.

"That explains what you're doing here," Grammy Robbins said to the firemen, "but it doesn't explain what *you* were doing in there." She turned to Nick.

"Hey, wait a minute," one of the firemen suddenly exclaimed, pointing to the casket, "if the chief's not in there, who did we carry out?"

Nick was at a loss for words. He wanted to explain everything to them, but he didn't know where to start. Finally he decided to start with Slim Jim. The crowd on the lawn grew silent when Nick knelt down and lifted the Embassy's lid. Looking up at Grammy, Nick tried to smile, hoping she would understand. That's when the photographer for the newspaper snapped the picture that would make the front page of the next day's *Wiloby Gazette*.

Chapter Eighteen

"He's going to kill me," Nick whispered to an ant that was climbing up his shoelace. It was Monday morning. Vincent had gone to the airport to pick up Aunt Marge and Uncle Walter. Nick was waiting in his hideout.

"I could run away to Florida or maybe Alaska," Nick said to the ant. "I've always wanted to go to Alaska and it would be fun to go ice fishing. I wonder if they have ants in Alaska." The ant was making its way across his sneaker. "I bet you'd freeze in Alaska." Then he wondered if he might freeze in Alaska, too. Aunt Marge had packed away his winter clothes and he didn't know where she had put them.

"Florida, it'll have to be Florida," Nick muttered, giving the ant a little nudge with his finger. "I can go deep-sea fishing there and find sharks' teeth on the beach. The only thing I'll need is my bathing suit." Nick knew where his bathing suit was, but somehow the thought of going all the way to Florida made him feel uneasy. Where would he sleep? And how would he eat? He sat thinking and watching as the ant hurried down his sneaker and onto a leaf on the ground.

Nick froze at the sound of a car pulling into the driveway. Holding his breath, he peeked out of the hideout to see his uncle's long black car. Vincent and Uncle Walter were sitting in the front seat and Aunt Marge was in the backseat. Nick watched as Grammy and Emily went down the stairs to meet them.

"What in heaven's name happened to the flowers around the fountain?" Uncle Walter demanded, slamming the car door. He and Aunt Marge hurried over to Grammy and Emily. When they all had gone into the house, Nick slipped out of his hideout and dashed over to the car. Vincent was unloading the suitcases.

"What did he say, Vince? Was he really mad?" Nick whispered, leaning on the car.

"He wasn't thrilled," Vincent said, shaking

his head. "He's hoping his insurance will cover the water damage from the sprinklers. It's a good thing for you that your grandmother called him at the hotel on Saturday. He's had the whole weekend to cool down. I didn't have the heart to tell him about the newspaper story, though."

"I should have run away," Nick moaned, covering his face with his hands. "He's going to kill me, I know he is."

"He's not going to kill you, Nick. Though it nearly killed *him* to hear about his rug and chairs getting all wet. Your uncle works hard to keep the place up. What you did wasn't right. You shouldn't have been fooling around in the chapel."

Nick bowed his head. "I wish I could take it all back," he said. "I just know he's going to kill me."

"No one is going to kill anyone." Uncle Walter's crisp voice snapped like a whip behind him. Nick spun around to see his uncle carrying the vase of wilted marigolds that Sam and Willie had picked for Slim Jim's service. Uncle Walter motioned for Vincent to take the suitcases into the house. Nick's stomach tightened. His uncle cleared his throat.

"I am not going to lose my temper and I

am not going to shout," Uncle Walter said, "because if I let myself lose my temper, I probably would kill you!" Nick winced at the sight of his uncle's reddening face. Uncle Walter took a deep breath and continued. "Vincent told us about the firemen mixing up the funeral homes on account of the fountain, and speaking of fountains, who was responsible for picking these?" He held up the vase of flowers.

"That was another mix-up," Nick tried to explain. "I told Sam and Willie to pick some flowers for the funeral . . ."

"Yes, and about this funeral," Uncle Walter interrupted. "Haven't I told you that playing in the chapel is strictly forbidden?" Nick nodded. "I'm very unhappy that you disobeyed me, Nick. I'm going to double your chores for the rest of the month. What made you think you could do such a thing? A snake! Emily said you were having a funeral for Bernard Trauffman's snake! Whatever possessed you?"

"Bernard was going to pay me."

"Pay you? You already get an allowance. Isn't that enough? Why do you need more money?" Uncle Walter demanded.

"I was going to use the money to buy *The*

Truckers' Road Atlas," Nick told him. "I never meant for all this to happen . . ."

"You are not to accept any money from Bernard or anyone else for that matter, where the funeral home is concerned," Uncle Walter snapped. "Do I make myself clear?"

"Very," Nick mumbled, choking back the tears.

"I am so disappointed in you. What in the world could you have done with a truckers' atlas, anyway? You're not even old enough to drive!"

"I will be someday," Nick said. The tears rolled down his cheeks. "And when I am, I'm going to get a truck just like my dad's and I'm going to drive as far away from here as I can. And I won't be around to disappoint you anymore." He closed his eyes and bit down on his lip to stop the tears. Suddenly, his uncle's arm was around his shoulders.

"You could have come to me, you know. If you wanted the atlas, I could have given you some work to earn the money you needed." There was a long silence before he continued. "I know it's been hard on you, Nick, not having your father alive, and I know that you resent me and the way I do things. I'm not your father and I never will be, but I was hoping that one day you'd see that having an uncle was the next best thing to a father. I think you need an uncle as much as I need a nephew."

Nick couldn't believe his ears. "You need a nephew?" he asked.

"Of course I do." Uncle Walter shook his head. "Without you, I'd be outnumbered by all the women in the house."

Nick looked up and saw that Uncle Walter was smiling.

"And I must say," Uncle Walter continued, "that your interest in the business is a surprise. From what Emily tells me, your friend Slim Jim had quite a service. I know you have your heart set on being a trucker like your dad, but if you ever change your mind, I think you could do a fine job helping me with the funeral home."

"You do?" Nick sputtered.

"Of course you need to work more on how to be responsible and conduct yourself in a proper way. In this business, proper conduct is very important. You have to learn to keep a low profile, with a certain amount of reserve. I think you could do it if you tried." Uncle Walter wrinkled his brow as he noticed some weeds that had sprouted up behind the Wiloby Funeral Home sign. "Let me just pull these up," he said. He stepped behind the sign and leaned over.

Just then Bernard and Ian came running down the sidewalk. Bernard was wearing a brand-new leather jacket. It looked very uncomfortable on such a hot morning.

"Hey, Nick, look at this," Ian called. Nick winced at the sight of the newspaper in his hand. "You and Slim made the front page!"

"I bet I'm the only kid whose pet got on the front page of a newspaper without being alive!" Bernard smirked.

"Shhh . . ." Nick tried to quiet them, but it was too late.

"What's this about the front page?" Uncle Walter asked. He stood up and reached for the paper. Bernard took a step backwards, and Ian scratched nervously at a scab on his knee.

Nick groaned. He had already seen the Sunday paper. There was a full-color picture of Slim Jim laid out in the Embassy. Nick and a group of firemen were smiling beside it. The headline read, "Firemen Find No Flames at Funeral, but Look Who's in the Casket!" Uncle Walter's face went white as he read the caption below the picture: "Weird goings-on at the Wiloby Funeral Home."

Nick cringed at the sound of his uncle's voice. "This is terrib . . ."

Suddenly the loud honk of an air horn filled the air.

"Hey, everybody," Vincent called, running down the sidewalk, "look who's here!"

Nick turned and saw the *Peach Blossom* pulling up to the curb.

Mr. Rafferty's head of bushy red hair was leaning out of the cab. "Hi, folks," he called, "how'd you like to meet your newest neighbor?" He opened the door and jumped out, hurrying over to the passenger side. Everyone broke into applause at the sight of Mrs. Rafferty stepping down from the cab. In her arms was a tiny bundle of blue blanket.

"It gives me the greatest pleasure," Mr. Rafferty beamed, "to introduce you to Vincent Walter Rafferty." Mrs. Rafferty lifted the blanket and revealed a tiny red face. Vincent and Uncle Walter stepped closer and the littlest Rafferty let out a squeak.

"Hey, he recognizes us!" Vincent cried. Everyone laughed and Uncle Walter blushed a deep red as Mrs. Rafferty reached over to kiss him. She kissed Vincent next, and he turned almost as red as Uncle Walter.

"I don't know how we would have managed without you," she said. Soon all the Rafferty kids came running out of their house and across the yard. The new baby was surrounded by his sisters and brothers and showered with kisses.

"My horoscope said that today I'd meet a very important person. I'm sure it must be you, Mr. Vincent Walter Rafferty," Grammy Robbins said. She and Aunt Marge and the girls accompanied Mrs. Rafferty and the baby to their house.

"I don't know how to thank you," Mr. Rafferty said, coming up to Uncle Walter and Vincent. "I'd like to do something to show our gratitude. If there's anything, anything at all I . . ."

"Well, now that you mention it . . ." Vincent said. He leaned over and whispered something in Uncle Walter's ear.

"Yes, there is something," Uncle Walter said. Then he whispered into Mr. Rafferty's ear. Nick wondered what all the whispering was about. Mr. Rafferty called Sam and Willie.

"Come on, we're going for a little ride," he

said. He climbed into the cab. The twins scrambled up behind him.

"So, what are you standing around for?" Vincent asked. He took hold of Nick's arm.

"They aren't going to wait all day for you," Uncle Walter said, grabbing his other arm. Before Nick could answer, Vincent and Uncle Walter hoisted him up to the open door.

The smell of diesel was in the air. Nick felt the hard leather seat below him. He was sitting high above the street. It was too good to be true, as if he had stepped into one of his best dreams. He was sitting in the cab of an eighteen-wheeler!

It's just the way I dreamed it would be, Nick thought. As he turned to look beside him, he felt a pang of disappointment. Something was wrong, something was missing. His father was nowhere in sight, and Mr. Rafferty was at the wheel. That's when Nick realized that one of his dreams could never come true.

Sam and Willie bobbed up and down excitedly as their father pulled away from the curb. Mr. Rafferty sang along with a country-and-western song that blasted out of the radio. Nick reached over to open the glove compartment, but there were no green lollipops inside. Instead, a number of maps and papers came spilling out. Nick bent down to pick them up.

"Hey! It's *The Truckers' Road Atlas!*" he cried, holding up a book of maps.

"Oh, you know about that?" Mr. Rafferty asked.

"I want to be a trucker when I grow up. I was going to send away for the atlas so that I could study the different routes," Nick told him, paging through the book, "but I don't have the money now."

"Tell you what," Mr. Rafferty said, "you can borrow mine. I've got enough maps to navigate my way to Mars. Besides, with the new baby here, I've decided not to make any long runs. I'll be staying close to home for a spell."

Nick couldn't believe his luck. Not only was he riding in a real eighteen-wheeler, but he had *The Truckers' Road Atlas,* too!

Meanwhile, Willie leaned forward and stuffed the rest of the maps back into the glove compartment. He found a stale bagel and tried to bite into it, but couldn't. Mr. Rafferty and Sam broke into laughter. Even Nick found himself giggling. Then the twins tried singing along with their father to the country tune, but they kept getting the words wrong, which caused more laughter. Before he knew it, Nick was laughing and singing along, too. He looked down at *The Truckers' Road Atlas* on his lap. Suddenly Vincent's words came rushing back to him: "You're going to have a lot of dreams, kiddo, and . . . they probably won't all come true." Nick listened to the Raffertys singing beside him. "And sometimes, when you follow a dream, you can get lucky and find yourself in a better place, even if it isn't exactly where you had hoped to go."

Nick smiled and leaned back against the seat. As they headed up Filmont Street he looked out the window. Bubs was running down the sidewalk after Moose, who had broken free from the leash. Aunt Marge, Emily, Grammy, and the rest of the Raffertys were waving from the Raffertys' front porch. Bernard and Ian were on the sidewalk. Bernard was sweating in his leather jacket and Ian was scratching at a mosquito bite on his arm. Vincent and Uncle Walter were waving in front of the Wiloby Funeral Home sign.

Nick waved back at them and giggled as he watched Moose sneak up to the fountain for a drink.

READ

The Castle in the Attic

Elizabeth Winthrop

A Yearling Book

Now available in all bookstores

ISBN: 0-440-40941-1 $3.99 U.S.
                                        $4.99 Canada

''Where did the castle come from? Tell me again,''
William said at dinner.

When they ate alone, they always sat in the kitchen.
The checkered curtains, the yeasty smell of Mrs. Phil-
lips's toast spread with Marmite, and the circle of light
that the green shaded lamp cast around them made
William feel cozy in the big, creaky house.

She did not settle into her seat until everything was
in place on the table: their plates, the salt and pepper,
honey for her tea, ketchup for his noodles, and chocolate syrup for his milk.

''I hate to get up in the middle of a meal,'' she said.

''You say that every night.''

''And I mean it every night.'' She poured some

honey into her tea. The floating spirals of gold slipped underneath the surface, one little circle after another. "Now about the castle. Every family has its own traditions that reach back into that family's history, into another time. Other people pass on Bibles or journals or old wedding dresses. My family has always passed on the castle. It goes back as far as my father's great-grandfather and probably to before that, although we don't have certain proof of it." She took a bite and chewed on it thoughtfully. "You remember when I went back to England last year?"

William nodded, his mouth full.

"I found the castle in my parents' house when my brother Richard and I were clearing it out. That's when I had it shipped to America."

"All the way from Stow-on-the-Wold, England?" said William. He used any excuse to roll that funny name around on his tongue.

"Now all the way to Riveredge Lane, Southbrook, New York, care of William Edward Lawrence, complete with drawbridge, chapel, armory, minstrels' gallery, and one Silver Knight. The tapioca pudding is in the icebox. None for me tonight."

He cleared the table and rinsed the plates. "What about the Silver Knight?" he asked, his voice raised over the running water. "Has he always been in the castle?"

"As far as I know. I think there might have been other soldiers originally because my great-grandfather mentioned some in a letter about the castle, but I've never seen them. When I was a child, there was only the Silver Knight. There was some legend that was passed down about him. I remember bits and pieces of it. He was thrown out of his kingdom long ago by an enemy of some sort, and it's said that one day he'll come back to life and return to reclaim his land. But the whole time I played with the castle, he was as stiff and cold as lead.''

William sat down again. He made paths in his pudding with his spoon before taking the first bite. He wasn't really listening to her story. The question of her leaving hung between them. It took up as much room at the table as he did.

''Afterward,'' he started, his voice almost choking on the word, ''will I have dinner alone on a night like this?''

''Oh, William,'' she said quietly. When he looked up, he saw tears in her eyes. ''Of course not. Don't you see, if I go now, your mother and father will spend more time with you. You and I, we're almost too close. It leaves other people out.''

''The castle doesn't make any difference,'' said William, getting up. ''I'm still going to figure out a way to make you stay.''